Dear Reader,

Readers sometimes wonder where I got my start as a writer. When I tell people that my first novels were romance novels for Bantam's Loveswept line, they're usually shocked. Although this genre may appear completely different from the suspense I write today, the two have more in common than it seems.

For me, there are two crucial elements to every good story: characters to fall in love with and root for, and a mystery to be solved, whether it is a crime or that baffling and bewildering emotion that puzzles us most of all—love. Even the most twisted murder plot can't compare to the complex inner workings of the human heart.

In *Keeping Company,* sensible corporate lawyer Alaina Montgomery has been frustrating her matchmaking friends for years. But this time they've *really* tried to set her up with the wrong guy: Dylan Harrison, a free-spirited single dad who runs a ramshackle bar and bait shop. Appropriately enough, she meets him on the way to a science-fiction-themed masquerade party. When cops mistake the costumed pair for a lady of the evening and her client, Alaina and Dylan end up in jail together. And soon they hatch a plan to foil the matchmakers once and for all by pretending to be a couple. What begins as a good-natured ruse quickly blossoms into a real romance, as these two polar opposites discover that desire can't be so easily disguised.

Dylan and Alaina's story brings us back to the small town featured in my Rainbow Chasers trilogy from years ago. I hope that you'll enjoy this story as much today as I did at the very beginning of my writing career.

All my best,

Tami Hoag

Tami Hoag

"Hoag certainly knows how to build a plot and her skill has deservedly landed her on bestseller lists numerous times." —*South Florida Sun-Sentinel*

"Hoag has a winner in this novel where she brings back Elena Estes.... Hoag is the consummate story-teller and creator of suspense." —*Mystery News*

"Tami Hoag weaves an intricate tale of murder and deception.... A very well-written and thought-out murder/mystery. Hoag is able to keep you guessing and you'll be left breathless until all the threads are unwoven and the killer is revealed." —Fresh Fiction

PRIOR BAD ACTS

"A snappy, scary thriller." —*Entertainment Weekly*

"Stunning ... Here [Hoag] stands above the competition, creating complex characters who evolve more than those in most thrillers. The breathtaking plot twists are perfectly paced in this compulsive page-turner." —*Publishers Weekly* (starred review)

"A chilling thriller with a romantic chaser." —New York *Daily News*

"A first-rate thriller with an ending that will knock your socks off." —*Booklist*

"An engrossing thriller with plenty of plot twists and a surprise ending." —*OK! Weekly*

"A chilling tale of murder and mayhem."
—*BookPage*

"The in-depth characterization and the unrelenting suspense are what makes [this] an outstanding read. Gritty and brutal at times, *Prior Bad Acts* delivers a stunning novel of murder, vengeance and retribution.... Riveting and chilling suspense."
—Romance Reviews Today

KILL THE MESSENGER

"Excellent pacing and an energetic plot heighten the suspense...enjoyable." —*Chicago Tribune*

"Everything rings true, from the zippy cop-shop banter, to the rebellious bike messenger subculture, to the ultimate, heady collision of Hollywood money, politics, and power."
—Minneapolis *Star Tribune*

"Hoag's usual crisp, uncluttered storytelling and her ability to make us care about her characters triumphs in *Kill the Messenger*."
—*South Florida Sun-Sentinel*

"A perfect book. It is well written, and it has everything a reader could hope for.... It cannot be put down.... Please don't miss this one."
—*Kingston Observer*

DARK HORSE

"A thriller as tightly wound as its heroine ... Hoag has created a winning central figure in Elena.... Bottom line: Great ride." —*People*

"This is her best to date.... [A] tautly told thriller." —Minneapolis *Star Tribune*

"Hoag proves once again why she is considered a queen of the crime thriller." —Charleston *Post and Courier*

"A tangled web of deceit and double-dealing makes for a fascinating look into the wealthy world of horses juxtaposed with the realistic introspection of one very troubled ex-cop. A definite winner." —*Booklist*

"Anyone who reads suspense novels regularly is acquainted with Hoag's work—or certainly should be. She's one of the most consistently superior suspense and romantic suspense writers on today's bestseller lists. A word of warning to readers: don't think you know whodunit 'til the very end." —Clute *Facts*

"Suspense, shocking violence, and a rip-roaring conclusion—this novel has all the pulse-racing touches that put Tami Hoag books on bestseller lists and crime fans' reading lists." —Baton Rouge *Advocate Magazine*

Books by Tami Hoag

TAMI HOAG

Keeping Company

BANTAM BOOKS
NEW YORK

Keeping Company is a work of fiction. Names, characters, places,
and incidents are the products of the author's imagination or are
used fictitiously. Any resemblance to actual events, locales, or
persons, living or dead, is entirely coincidental.

2010 Bantam Books Mass Market Edition

Published in the United States by Bantam Books,
an imprint of The Random House Publishing Group,
a division of Random House, Inc., New York.

BANTAM BOOKS and the rooster colophon
are registered trademarks of Random House, Inc.

Originally published in mass market in the United States in
paperback by Bantam Books, a division of Random House, Inc.,
in 1990.

ISBN 978-0-553-80641-0

Cover art: Image Source/Getty Images

Printed in the United States of America

www.bantamdell.com

2 4 6 8 9 7 5 3 1

Keeping
Company

Prologue

❦

University of Notre Dame, South Bend, Indiana
Spring 1977

"Okay, everybody, this is it. The final portrait of the Fearsome Foursome. Make sure your caps are on straight, ladies. I'm setting the timer now." Bryan Hennessy hunched over the 35-millimeter camera, fussing with buttons and switches, pausing once to push his glasses up on his straight nose.

Alaina Montgomery took a deep breath and slowly released it, trying to will the tension from her body. It would be hours before she would have to confront her mother—and stepfather number three, Bernie, the wheezing orthodontist. This moment was for her friends.

Decked out in graduation caps and gowns, they stood on the damp grass near the blue expanse of St. Mary's Lake. The clean, cool air was sweet with the scents of spring flowers, new leaves, and freshly cut grass. Birdsong mingled with Alice Cooper's "School's Out" blasting from a boom box in a distant dorm.

To her left stood Faith Kincaid, their very own Pollyanna—blond, innocent, and diplomatic. At the other end of the line stood petite Jayne Jordan, all wide eyes and wild auburn hair—their resident flake. Bryan hustled around to stand behind them, his cap askew. He was tall and athletic with a handsome, honest face and shaggy tawny hair. He was sweet and eccentric—their surrogate big brother, their confidant.

These were Alaina's three best friends in the world. In many respects they were her family, the only people she had ever allowed to get closer than an emotional arm's length away from her.

They had banded together their freshman year. Four people with nothing in common but a class in medieval sociology. Over the four years that followed they had seen each other through finals and failures, triumphs and tragedies, and doomed romances. They were friends in the truest, deepest sense of the word.

And today they would graduate and go their separate ways.

The hollow feeling that thought brought on scared the hell out of Alaina, and she frowned at the weakness as she reached up to check the state of her sensibly short chestnut hair.

"Okay, everybody smile," Bryan ordered, his voice a little huskier than usual. "It's going to go off any second now. Any second."

They all grinned engagingly and held their collective breaths.

The camera suddenly tilted downward on its tripod, pointing its lens at one of the white geese that wandered freely around St. Mary's Lake. The shutter clicked, and the motor advanced the film. The goose honked an outraged protest and waddled away.

"I hope that's not an omen," Jayne said, frowning as she nibbled at her thumbnail.

"It's a loose screw," Bryan announced, digging a dime out of his pants pocket to repair the tripod with.

"In Jayne or the camera?" Alaina queried, her cool blue eyes sparkling with teasing mischief.

Jayne made a face. "Very funny, Alaina."

"I think it's a sign that Bryan needs a new tripod," said Faith.

"That's not what Jessica Porter says," Alaina remarked slyly.

The girls giggled as Bryan's blush crept up to the roots of his hair. While there had never been any romantic developments within their ranks, outside of his unusual friendship with the three of them, Alaina knew Bryan had an active social life. She was going to miss teasing him about it.

"If you want a sign, look behind you," Bryan said as he fussed unnecessarily with the aperture setting on the camera.

They turned together and immediately caught sight of the rainbow that arched gracefully across the morning sky above the golden dome of the administration building.

"Oh, how beautiful," Faith said with a sigh.

"Symbolic," Jayne whispered.

"It's the diffusion of light through raindrops," Alaina said flatly, crossing her arms in front of her. She had always been the practical anchor of the group. It was a role she had no intention of giving up. She proudly vowed there wasn't a romantic bone in her body.

Bryan looked up from fiddling with the camera to frown at her, his strong jaw jutting forward aggressively. "Rainbows have lots of magic in them," he said, dead serious. "Ask any leprechaun. It'd do you some good to believe in magic, Alaina."

Alaina's lush mouth turned down at the corners. It wasn't the first time they'd had this argument, but it was probably going to be the last. A sharp pang reverberated throughout the hollowness inside her chest. She swallowed hard. "Take the picture, Hennessy."

Bryan ignored her, his wise, warm blue eyes taking on a dreamy quality as he gazed up at the soft stripes of color. "We'll each be chasing our own rainbows after today. I wonder where they'll lead us."

They each recited the stock answers they'd

been giving faculty, friends, and family for months. Jayne was leaving to seek fame and fortune in Hollywood as a writer and director. Bryan had been accepted into the graduate program of parapsychology at Purdue. Faith was headed to a managerial position in a business office in Cincinnati. Alaina was staying on at Notre Dame to attend law school.

"That's where our brains are taking us," Bryan said, pulling his cap off to comb a hand back through his hair as he always did when he went into one of his "deep thinking modes." "I wonder where our hearts will take us."

If anyone knew the answer to that, it was Bryan, Alaina thought. He was the one they told all their secrets to. He was the only person on earth who knew her deepest wish was for security—not just financial security, but emotional security. And he was the only one who knew just how afraid she was to pursue that dream. Hell, she seldom admitted it to herself. Jayne and Faith would probably have been stunned to know strong, self-sufficient Alaina was afraid of anything, but Bryan's reaction had been understanding. More than once she had wished he really was her brother, that she could have had his support while she'd been growing up in a house devoid of emotion.

"That's the question we should all be asking ourselves." Jayne wagged a slender finger at her friends. "Are we in pursuit of our true bliss, or are we merely following a course charted by the expectations of others?"

"Do we have to get philosophical?" Alaina groaned, rubbing two fingers on each throbbing temple. "I haven't had my mandatory ten cups of coffee yet this morning."

"Life is philosophy, honey," Jayne explained patiently, her voice a slow Kentucky drawl that hadn't altered one iota during the four years she'd spent in northern Indiana. The expression on her delicately sculpted features was almost comically earnest. "That's a cosmic reality."

Alaina blinked. Jayne was her opposite in nearly every way. It was amazing they had become such close friends. Finally Alaina said, "We don't have to worry about you. You'll fit right in in California."

Jayne smiled. "Why, thank you."

Faith chuckled. "Give up, Alaina. You can't win."

Alaina winced and held her hands up as if to ward off the words. "Don't say that. I *abhor* losing."

"Anastasia," Bryan declared loudly. He gave a decisive nod that set the tassel on his cap dancing. The statement would have seemed straight out of left field to anyone who didn't know Bryan Hennessy and the workings of his unconventional mind.

Anastasia was the small town on California's rugged northern coast where the four of them had spent spring break. Alaina's lips tilted in a rueful smile at the memory of the fantasy plans they had made to move there and pursue idealistic existences. Jayne's dream had been to have her own farm. Bryan had wanted to play the role of local mad scientist. An inn with a view of the ocean had been Faith's wish. They had somehow gotten Alaina to admit to a secret desire to paint.

"That's right," Faith said with a misty smile. "We'd all move to Anastasia."

"And live happily ever after." Alaina's tone lacked the sarcasm she had intended. She sounded wistful instead.

"Even if we never end up there, it's a nice dream," Jayne said softly.

A nice dream. Something to hang on to, like their memories of Notre Dame and each other. Warm, golden images they could hold in a secret place in their hearts to be taken out from time to time when they were feeling lonely or blue.

The hollowness seemed to grow within Alaina at the thought, and she had to blink back the embarrassing beginnings of tears. She *wasn't* nostalgic, and she *wouldn't* cry.

Bryan set the timer on the camera once again and jogged around to stand behind Faith. "Who knows? Life is full of crossroads. You can never tell where a path might lead to."

And the camera buzzed and clicked, capturing the Fearsome Foursome—wishful smiles canting their mouths, dreams of the future and tears of parting shining in their eyes as a rainbow arched in the sky behind them—on film for all time.

Chapter 1

It was a dark and stormy night.

Only Jayne Jordan had a flair for the dramatic so strong that she could somehow manage to get Mother Nature to cooperate with her party plans, Alaina thought. She stared through the windshield of her BMW at the clouds scudding across the face of the full moon. It seemed a perfect night for a science fiction theme party.

Not that Alaina knew the first thing about science fiction. She couldn't think of the last time she'd read something that wasn't written in legalese. Of course, she wouldn't have read science fiction if she'd been stranded on a desert island with nothing but a carton of those novels. She was far too sensible for that sort of thing.

She piloted her car down the road that snaked along the coastal cliffs north of Anastasia, California. If it weren't for the fact that she was absolutely practical and levelheaded, she might have been feeling a little nervous. She was alone on a dark stretch of road, dressed up in a ridiculous costume on her way to a theme party. If this were a movie, she thought, now would be the time for the car to break down.

"Don't be silly, Alaina," she muttered as her elegant, meticulously manicured hands unconsciously clenched the leather-padded steering wheel.

She was never silly. Maybe once—okay, twice—in her entire life had she been silly. The first time had involved earthworms and she had been only five years old. The second time had been recently, and as the handsome face of A. Clayton Collier flashed through her memory, Alaina gritted her even white teeth and resolutely shoved the incident from her mind.

She wasn't going to be silly now. She was going

to go to Jayne's party and put in her required appearance because Jayne was a dear friend despite the fact that she had sent Alaina this absurd costume and insisted she wear it. Occasionally one had to humor Jayne Jordan's sense of whimsy or be nagged about it for the rest of one's life. Since they were now living in the same area, it seemed only prudent to indulge her. But if any potential clients saw her in this getup...

Not much chance of that, she decided. The majority of Jayne's friends were not likely to seek legal counsel. They were more apt to consult psychics and palmists.

She would put in her appearance, stay the minimum time that could be considered socially acceptable, and drive back into Anastasia to her new home—a renovated Victorian duplex that sat on a hill with a lovely view of the marina. She would put a Mozart disc in the CD player, pour herself a glass of Chivas Regal, and maybe work a little on the painting she had begun that morning. It would be a very relaxing evening.

That had been the whole idea behind her move from Chicago to California five months before.

To get away from the whirlwind pace she had maintained at the prestigious law offices of Abercrombie, Turtletaub, and Flinch, to regain some perspective on what she really wanted in life, to forget—

The thought slammed into the granite wall of her will before it could completely form. A. Clayton Collier had done a really crummy thing, stringing her along, letting her believe his divorce was all but finalized when he hadn't so much as broached the topic with his wife. But that didn't mean she had to think about it. No. The incident meant less than nothing to her. Clayton had been a dalliance, a fling. What he'd done hadn't broken her heart. Absolutely not, Alaina vowed, ignoring the wrenching ache in her chest.

She was a sophisticated woman, a career woman, a woman of the nineties. She cherished her freedom. She didn't have a care in the world.

The words had no sooner crossed her mind than her car abruptly died. Alaina pumped the accelerator furiously, but the BMW only slowed until she was forced to steer it off the road onto a graveled scenic-overlook area. The car rolled to a halt, and Alaina sat in the gloom, staring in stunned disbelief at the lighted instrument panel, feeling utterly betrayed.

This was one of the finest cars money could buy. It had every option, every luxury, everything including the love and adoration of its owner. And it had just stranded her in the middle of bloody nowhere.

"Lovely," Alaina grumbled. "Just lovely."

Sitting back against the plush leather seat, she took a deep breath and released it slowly, schooling her temper. This sort of thing required a cool head. She would simply have to walk back to Anastasia and call a tow truck.

She slung her purse over her shoulder and climbed out of the car, but when she turned to start her hike, the resolve washed out of her on a sigh of defeat. The lights of the little town winked a good two miles in the distance—a marathon-length walk in three-inch glittering silver spike heels.

Leaning against the roof of the car, she ran a hand back through her dark hair. As promised, the fifty-dollar, precision-cut, chin-length style fell back into place with artless simplicity. She stared out at the ocean that rippled like liquid ebony beneath the night sky. The wind howled. Below the cliff the surf pounded against the shore.

Brother, this is eerie, she thought, her skin crawling beneath the thin fabric of her dress. Her imagination turned again to movies. She was no expert on B-grade horror flicks—Jayne was the critic—but wasn't this the part where the escaped lunatic came wandering out of the fog?

He could think of any number of things he would rather be doing. Spending the evening with his children, going over the monthly report for his business, having gum surgery.

"Snap out of it," Dylan Harrison ordered himself as he slowed the Bronco, shifting down for a hairpin curve.

Ordinarily he would have been the life of the party. Especially when the party had a science fiction theme. He was, after all, something of an expert on the genre. But tonight was different. Tonight he turned forty.

He'd never been one to worry about age. Depression over this particular birthday had sort of snuck up on him. It wasn't so much that he minded being forty years old. It was that his friends minded his being forty years old—and unmarried.

He cringed at the thought of what lay ahead for him at the party. Who would Jayne try to fix him up with this time? The platinum blonde who designed dangerous-looking sheet-metal jewelry and secretly admitted to being a druid priestess? Or would it be the man-crazy Babbette, proprietor of the local hypnosis and suntanning parlor?

It really was good to have such caring friends, Dylan thought sincerely. Jayne's matchmaking efforts stemmed from a genuine concern. He only wished his caring friends would realize that he was perfectly happy. He liked his life the way it was—uncomplicated—and he liked himself the way he was—unambitious, unmarried.

In fact, it was because he wanted his life uncomplicated that he was unambitious and unmarried. He'd taken his taste of the yuppie lifestyle. He'd given his all to his job as an investment counselor, devoted himself to acquiring the material trappings of the upwardly mobile. He and Veronica had had it all—a Volvo, a PC, a CD, a Cuisinart, a coffee bean grinder, Southwestern decor. Now Veronica had all those things, and Dylan had what mattered to him—his children and his sanity.

In Anastasia he was free to be himself. No matter how offbeat he chose to be, his friends here liked him just fine. And he treasured them. If only they'd stop trying to marry him off.

He steered the Bronco around another curve in the road, and suddenly there she was. She was a vision. She was perfection. Holy Hannah, it was Andora in the flesh! Princess Andora of the Zanatares, Star Commander of the Seventh Galaxy Fleet, dream lover of every male this side of the Milky Way.

Dylan's heart thumped in his chest as he guided his Bronco off the highway and onto the shoulder. Gravel crunched beneath the tires as he pulled in behind the BMW. Apparently the princess had expensive taste even when visiting Earth, he thought with a wry smile. That was the one thing that had always bothered him about Andora—she was a materialist.

The headlights illuminated her in an aura of amber light. She was lovely—no, breathtaking, he amended, his gaze lingering on the long, *long* legs encased in dark fishnet stockings. Her uniform was impeccable—short enough to make a man hyperventilate, but impeccable nevertheless. And it appeared to be absolutely authentic. He wondered where she had come by it. He was always on the lookout for genuine finds to add to his extensive collection of science fiction memorabilia, and he had never run across a Princess Andora costume that even came close to this one. Of course, having that world-class body in the uniform probably added considerably to its authenticity.

The dress was made of a metallic-silver fabric—especially handwoven for the princess by the albino Nymphads of Lydon's moon desert, according to Andora's creator, H.M.W. Wilmott. It bared the woman's regal shoulders, displayed to perfection her high, full breasts, hugged her slender waist and womanly hips, and ended in a flounced skirt at the very top of her—Dylan sighed again—long, *long* legs.

The princess smiled at him as he climbed down out of the truck. Her lush mouth lifted wryly, kicking up a little higher on the right. Her features were elegant, almost patrician. The comic-book character of Andora had been Dylan's image of an ideal woman since he'd read his first issue during puberty. This real-life woman was the personification of that image. A man couldn't ask for a better fortieth-birthday present, he decided. She was a dream come true—a science fiction aficionado with the gams of a goddess.

Dylan raised his left arm in a proper Zanatarian salute. "Greetings, Princess Andora!" he said, assuming she would be suitably impressed by his vast knowledge of the character she had chosen to portray. "All hail supreme ruler of the Zanatares!"

Alaina's face froze, and her smile died a pitiful death. "Oh, my Lord," she mumbled, pressing an icy-cold hand to her racing heart. "He *is* a lunatic."

It was a shame, really, she thought as she stared at the man walking toward her. He was handsome, *very* handsome, though she admitted the light was bad. It hardly seemed right for such good looks to be wasted on a maniac. Tall and rangy, he had a long, lean face with a bold nose and a square chin. The wind raked through his wavy, dark hair, then he clamped a wide-brimmed hat on his head, tilting it to a jaunty angle over his right eye.

He was dressed very strangely. But then Alaina supposed lunatics weren't given accounts at the better men's stores even in California. He wore knee-high boots and baggy pants, and what could only be described as a frock coat with a waistcoat beneath it, and a white shirt with question marks embroidered on the points of the collar. His neck was wrapped with an amazingly long, knitted scarf, the ends of which hung well past his knees.

"Has Volton accompanied you, my lady, or are you without escort on this planet?" he asked in a smooth, resonant baritone voice.

"I'm going to die a cheap, horror-movie death," Alaina mumbled, stunned by the prospect and more than a little miffed. It wasn't at all the end she would have pictured for herself.

20

Well, she decided, squaring her shoulders, she would go with dignity, and she would damn well know who her killer was—provided he would tell her. It wasn't as if she could demand the information at gunpoint. The most dangerous weapon she had with her was her tongue. It had cut opposing attorneys to ribbons in the courtroom, but she doubted it would have much of an impact on a lunatic.

"Who are you?" she demanded in her coolest, haughtiest tone.

"Precisely." Dylan grinned and nodded. She'd recognized him right off. The woman knew her stuff.

Alaina's elegant eyebrows pulled together in annoyed confusion. "Precisely what?"

"Who."

"Who?"

"Yes." He dug a hand into the pocket of his coat and produced a small white bag, which he offered to Alaina. "Jelly Baby?"

Cautiously, she peered into the bag. They may have looked like ordinary, everyday jelly beans, but they were undoubtedly drugged. Scowling, she planted her hands on her hips. "You scum. This stuff is destroying the fabric of American society, and you couldn't care less."

Dylan looked in the bag as if its contents might have undergone some evil metamorphosis. Nope. They were just jelly beans. He gave the princess a quizzical look. "You think jelly beans are destroying the fabric of American society? Wow. You must have been raised by a pack of dentists."

Alaina narrowed her eyes and blatantly ignored his inane prattle. No simpleminded psychotic was going to get the better of her! "You may think you're going to kill me, but I'm not going to make it easy for you!"

"Time Lords have nothing against the Zanatares," Dylan said, extremely puzzled. She should have known that. "Why would I want to kill you?"

Alaina's control slipped a notch as her temper rose. She flapped her arms at her sides in an exasperated shrug. "Because you're a lunatic!"

Dylan's straight brows shot up in surprise. He must have missed an episode of Andora's exploits somewhere along the line. "I am?"

Alaina huffed indignantly, not appreciating the fact that he would question her judgment on this matter. "It seems obvious to me!"

Dylan rubbed his chin. He was fairly certain she was wrong—genre-wise. Personally, he cultivated an unorthodox image, but no one had ever called him a lunatic except Veronica. Maybe this lovely princess was a bit unbalanced—a good bet if she was a friend of Jayne's—but she had fire and spunk... and long, *long* legs. And when she huffed and puffed like that, her breasts did the most amazing kind of synchronized dance and her metallic bodice shimmered in the harsh glow of the headlights.

"Well, just look at you." She made an impatient gesture of annoyed disgust. "You're dressed like—like—a pimp from another planet! And sane people don't go around spouting crazy nonsense about princesses and Time Lords, trying to give people drugs and—"

"Crazy nonsense?"

Dylan suddenly felt the lightbulb go on above his head, and he gave a shout of laughter that made the woman before him jump back against her car.

Alaina's eyes narrowed in suspicion. "What's so funny?"

"You don't know who you are!" he exclaimed between gasps of laughter.

"I'm perfectly well aware of who I am," she insisted. "I don't know who *you* are!"

Dylan doubled over in a renewed fit of laughter, knowing she wouldn't understand why, but unable to control himself. *Who* was exactly who he was—*Dr.* Who, the lead character of the wildly popular British television science fiction series. This gorgeous woman was in Princess Andora's costume, but it was clear she didn't know Andora from Adam, and she probably thought Time Lords were a rock group!

It was too funny. No wonder the poor creature thought he was demented! She didn't know beans about science fiction, while he had assumed she was as big a fan of the genre as he was himself!

Blue eyes wide and wary, Alaina plastered herself back against the side of her car and watched him as tears streamed down his cheeks. His hat fell off and landed on the gravel in front of his big booted feet as he cackled like—well, like a maniac.

Now was her chance. He was distracted by his own lunacy. If she could just hit him over the head with something or—Mace! She had a can of Mace in her purse! If she could just get it out and if it hadn't gone flat or something. She'd been carrying it around with her for at least a decade, ever ready to blast the odd rapist or mugger. She tore open her Gucci handbag and began digging through it.

Dylan finally managed to get hold of himself. By now the poor woman had to think he was completely bonkers. It was time to set her straight and let her know he was more or less a regular guy. Once they'd sorted through the misunderstanding, he could offer her a ride to Jayne Jordan's party. That was obviously what she was dressed for, even though she wasn't familiar with the character she was playing.

Straightening, he wiped at his eyes, and his gaze focused on the woman before him. She was rummaging through her designer handbag with a purposeful look on her lovely face. "What are you doing?"

"Never mind," Alaina mumbled. She pulled out her calfskin wallet, a comb, a pack of cigarettes, and her monogrammed gold lighter, and thrust the lot of it at her assailant. "Hold this," she commanded.

Dylan grabbed the stuff in a reflex action and watched in fascination as she continued her search. "Looking for something in particular, Princess?"

"Yes. My Mace. Here it is!" she exclaimed triumphantly.

Shouting an expletive, Dylan flung the things Alaina had handed him into the air. Lunging forward, he pinned her flat against the side of the BMW before she could extract the slim canister from her purse.

"Are you crazy?" he asked, his face mere inches from hers. In her stiletto heels, she was very nearly as tall as he was—two inches over six feet. Matched so evenly, their bodies fit together like two halves of a whole, a fact that had a very distracting effect on his brain.

"No, *you* are," she retorted. "I think we've already established that fact."

"Lady, you're not making any sense at all," Dylan complained somewhat absently, conveniently forgetting that he had been speaking what must have seemed to her to be a foreign language up to this point. His quick wit was wandering... all over Andora.

Warmth flashed beneath the surface of his skin as she shifted against him. Nuts or not, Princess Andora had one hell of a body, and strategic parts of it were melting beneath strategic parts of his. His anger evaporated in the heat of sudden desire.

"*I'm* not making sense?" Alaina questioned, her husky alto reduced to little more than a hoarse, indignant whisper.

She should have been terrified, but she wasn't. She didn't really feel threatened by him. She felt...something else altogether. A strange wave of confusion rippled through her normally sharp mind as equally strange tingles ran through her body. Under that weird getup this crazy guy had some kind of physique! The thighs that flanked hers were solid muscle. So was the chest that was pressed to her own, flattening her suddenly sensitive breasts. Her gaze fixed on his mouth, and she wondered dazedly why God would put such sexy lips on a maniac. They were cut just right—not too thick, not too thin—and perfectly arranged on his wide mouth. And they looked firm and kissable.

"No," Dylan muttered, his eyes magnetically drawn to the beautiful upper slopes of her breasts, which were accommodatingly bared by the neckline of her costume. Who was he to accuse anybody of not making sense? Staring at Princess Andora was unleashing a sensual fog in his own brain that could have put London's to shame. Still, she was the root of the problem. "You're not making a bit of sense. What are you, a lawyer?"

That cleared her head. Alaina gasped in outrage, further heaving her cleavage up beneath the man's nose. "Just what kind of a crack is that?"

"Oh, no." Dylan groaned, making a face. The tide of disappointment left him feeling weak. Without thinking, he sagged a little deeper into the exotic-smelling feminine form he had sandwiched against the car. All these lush curves on an attorney. What a waste! What use did a lawyer have for ripe breasts?

Her heart sinking along with her temper, Alaina tried to swallow down the knot in her throat. She felt the oddest sense of blighted hope. But what had she been hoping for? She wasn't in the market for a man.

Shoving the question aside, she considered her situation. Just her luck. She had to be attacked by a lunatic who had a beef with lawyers! He'd probably been committed to the nut hatch by one. Who could imagine the atrocities running rampant through the man's maladjusted mind? He'd no doubt been dreaming up sordid forms of revenge all during the course of his incarceration.

"This is so humiliating," she muttered, more to herself than to him as her anger reached the boiling point. "I'm a member of Phi Beta Kappa. I graduated with honors from Notre Dame. I was the youngest partner in the history of Abercrombie, Turtletaub, and Flinch. I had an apartment on Lake Shore Drive that people would sell their children for. And I threw it all away to move here, only to be murdered by a poorly dressed maniac!"

"I am not going to kill you," Dylan announced. "Lord knows, the world would be a better place with fewer lawyers in it, but I'm not going to kill you."

"Ha! Not in front of a cop, at any rate!" Alaina's eyes lit up as her gaze fastened on the squad car that was pulling to the side of the road. She gave the man a malicious grin. "You're in for it now, Jack. They're going to put you away until your teeth fall out."

He rolled his eyes as he stepped back from her and planted his hands on his lean hips.

The deputy emerged from the car slowly, making a great show of sliding his nightstick into his wide belt and adjusting his hat. He was plump and jowly and looked like Jonathan Winters in a khaki uniform.

"Deputy," Alaina said, heaving a huge sigh of relief that made her breasts jump and fall. "Thank God you happened along."

"I wouldn't think you'd be so glad to see me," the man said with a rude snort.

"You know her?" Dylan asked, hooking a thumb in Alaina's direction.

"I know her kind," the deputy answered in a Joe Friday monotone. He stuck his thumbs behind his belt buckle and rocked back on his heels, nodding sagely. "They're pretty much all alike."

"You can say that again." Career women. Dylan shuddered. He should have taken one look at that BMW and run like hell.

The cop shot him a look. "You ought to know, huh, bub?"

"You can say that again." Obviously the deputy had heard about his divorce from TV news anchorwoman, Veronica Howard. Yes, he knew all about career women.

The deputy swaggered a step or two closer to Alaina, his stern gaze running from the top of her head to the tip of her sparkly silver shoes. "Okay, sweetheart, what's the story? Holding out money on your boss here, so he decided to rough you up, huh? It's an old story. I've heard it told a hundred times. A nice girl goes bad and falls in with a bum who makes his money off women and depravity. Makes me sick."

Alaina stared at him for a full thirty seconds before comprehension dawned. Slowly her own gaze slid down the front of her, taking in the low-cut, body-hugging, thigh-length, metallic-silver dress. That was bad enough, but then there were the mesh stockings and the stilt shoes.

Oh, Lord, she groaned inwardly, the man thought she was a hooker!

"This isn't what you think," she said primly, discreetly tugging up the bodice of her costume and wishing for the millionth time in her life that she didn't have such a generous bosom. "I'm an attorney."

"And I'm Mickey Spillane." He pulled a notebook from his breast pocket and wet the tip of his pencil with his tongue. "Name?"

"She's Princess Andora of the Zanatares," Dylan said, completely unconcerned about the situation and more than a little amused by the black look Alaina shot his way. "Don't you recognize her?"

The deputy frowned at him. "Who are you?"

Dylan grinned, pushing back the tails of his frock coat and tucking his hands into the pockets of his baggy pants. "Yes, I am."

"Yes, you are who?"

"Absolutely."

Alaina quickly bent and snatched up her cigarettes and lighter. She shook one out of the pack and planted it between her lips. "Can we please dispense with the Abbott and Costello routine?" she said dryly as she lit up. "We've already done Who's on First."

The deputy shook his pencil at Dylan. "Don't get cute with me, bub. I'll flatten you like yesterday's roadkill. I'll shake you so hard, your kids'll come out dizzy."

Dylan's brows lifted. He fought back a smile. This guy belonged on a sitcom. But then, this entire scene belonged on a sitcom. It was just the sort of situation that appealed to his sense of the absurd. "You're new around here, aren't you?"

"Don't think that's gonna help you, pal. I'm not some green-as-grass rookie. I've been around the block. I know the score. I've seen the mean streets."

Taking a deep drag on her cigarette, Alaina just barely managed not to groan. She squinted at the deputy's chest, trying to make out his name tag in the glare of two sets of headlights. "Look, Deputy Screwup—"

"That's Skrea-wupp," he corrected her stiffly. "It's Flemish."

Alaina bit her tongue, then pressed on with her usual aplomb, as if she hadn't just made a monumental blunder. "How fascinating. Please allow me to explain what happened here. I was on my way to a friend's party when my car broke down and this lunatic tried to attack me."

Dylan's look was incredulous. "I did not try to attack you!"

"So, you finally admit you're a lunatic," Alaina said, jumping on his careless omission. "Now we're getting somewhere!"

"Yeah," Deputy Skreawupp drawled, pulling out a pair of handcuffs. "Now we're getting in the squad car and going to the station. You're both under arrest."

Alaina shot him her most imperious glare, knowing the effect was somewhat lost, what with her standing there dressed like a cheap thrill. Still, she had to make the effort. She had a reputation to protect. "You have got to be kidding."

"You're making a big mistake," Dylan chimed in.

"You have the right to remain silent."

Chapter 2

The Anastasia jail was an unusually pleasant sort of place. Housed in an old stone building two blocks off the waterfront, the interior had been completely remodeled. The walls were painted white, and there was a mural done in pastels depicting a sailing scene and the annual migration of the gray whales behind the front desk. All in all, Alaina thought it looked more like the Chamber of Commerce office than a jail.

They were greeted by a smiling, cherub-faced lady in her fifties who wore a surfing T-shirt and a button that encouraged everyone to HAVE A NICE DAY IN ANASTASIA. When she glanced up from her paperwork, she beamed at the man handcuffed to Alaina's left arm.

"Why, hello, Dylan! What are you doing here?"

Deputy Skreawupp peered over their shoulders. "Disturbing the peace, simple assault, and conspiracy to solicit."

"Goodness!" the woman said, chuckling, her blue eyes shining like sapphires. "You've been a busy boy tonight!"

"This is all a simple misunderstanding, Jan," Dylan said. His good humor had returned on the ride into town. The whole thing could be cleared up in no time, and he had to admit he had sort of enjoyed watching Ms. Career Woman hiss and sputter in the squad car. It had been a double treat, considering what she was wearing.

Even now he couldn't help but glance at her standing there beside him, mad as a wet cat, her arctic-blue eyes shooting daggers at everyone and everything in their path. She made one hell of a Princess Andora—regal, aristocratic, fiery. Not to mention well endowed, he thought as his gaze strayed to her heaving cleavage.

A rueful little sigh slipped through his lips at

the thought that she was exactly the kind of woman he had taken a blood oath to avoid for the rest of his life. True, he had known her for less than an hour, but the warning signs were there glaring at him with neon intensity. An attorney with an attitude and a BMW. The car had tipped him off straightaway. In his book, BMW stood for Business-Minded Woman—something he'd had his fill of during the last turbulent year of his marriage to Veronica.

"You know this man, Mrs. Fletcher?" the deputy asked.

"Oh, my, yes!" the woman behind the counter said. "This is Dylan Harrison. He runs Dylan's Bar and Bait Shop down at the marina. Dylan, this is Deputy Skreawupp."

Dylan nodded, raising his handcuffed right hand and dragging Alaina's left one up with it. "Yes, we've met."

Mrs. Fletcher's little mouth turned down in a worried frown. "Dear." Then her gaze settled on Alaina, or more to the point, on Alaina's outfit, and her frown deepened to almost comic proportions.

A blush bloomed on the apples of her chubby cheeks. "Ohhhh, dear."

Alaina ignored the woman and turned on the deputy, fixing him with a furious glare. "I demand you take these handcuffs off immediately unless you want harassment charges heaped on top of false arrest."

Deputy Skreawupp glared back at her, his double chins set at a stubborn angle. "This is a righteous bust, sweet cheeks."

"I was *not* disturbing the peace."

Dylan waggled his eyebrows and did his best Groucho imitation. "You were certainly disturbing *my* peace."

Alaina followed his pointed gaze to the plunging neckline of her dress. A blush crept up from beneath it all the way to the roots of her hair. Ordinarily, she would have had a scathing put-down for the man, but not one sensible word came to her mind. His hot, glittering brown eyes had suddenly thrown her into some kind of weird hormonal meltdown.

Their gazes collided when she looked up, and the awareness that sizzled between them nearly knocked her off her spike heels. Then Dylan smiled and winked at her, and Alaina felt her knees sway. *This is weird,* she thought. She would have called any other man a sexist pig and smacked him one for looking at her that way. But Dylan Harrison's gaze didn't leave her feeling insulted. She felt strangely... hmmm, what was the word? Flattered? Attracted? Confused.

How she could be attracted to the man was quite beyond her. He had gotten her arrested, for Pete's sake! And the man was unquestionably certifiable. The fact that he had great cheekbones and the sexiest mouth she'd ever seen didn't enter into it. The fact that he had a voice like warm silk was of no consequence. He had a pierced ear and no regard for proper behavior or fashion. How could she, Alaina Montgomery, consummate yuppie, levelheaded woman of the world, be attracted to such a man?

She couldn't. But she was. And the twinkle in his eye told her he knew it.

"I'll take the cuffs off," the deputy said reluctantly, producing a key from his trouser pocket, "but no funny stuff. One wrong move from either one of you, and I'll stop you like a cheap watch."

Dylan's mouth twitched—an action Alaina couldn't help but catch since she was staring at the firm, sharp cut of his lips. A giggle bubbled up inside her, stunning her into frowning. What did she have to laugh about? She was supposed to be furious!

She shot Dylan a scowl as they followed the deputy through the little gate into the area behind the front counter, where old wooden chairs lined one wall and plain metal desks took up the floor space.

"On what grounds are you arresting me?" she asked the deputy.

"I'd say that dress is probable cause to make a man do just about anything," Dylan murmured, tilting his head down near hers so only she could hear him.

His low voice rolled over her skin like a sensual wave. Alaina shivered as her suddenly wild imagination conjured up intimate images—that voice floating to her ears across the width of a pillow in a moon-bright room. She could practically hear the sheets rustle. It was all she could do to keep herself from swaying toward the source of that silky voice. The handcuffs had been removed, but Dylan remained close enough so she could feel the natural heat of his body. His warmth attracted her like a magnet.

What was the matter with her? she wondered frantically, what seemed to be the last of her sanity digging its heels in for one last stand. She didn't react this way to men. Her *mother* reacted this way to men.

An irrational fear grabbed her by the throat at the thought that she was showing signs of suddenly turning into a clone of her mother. Lord, first there had been that business with A.—for adultery—Clayton Collier. She should have somehow known that he was married. There must have been signs, but she hadn't heeded them. Now this bizarre attraction to a man wearing an earring, a man who ran a bar and bait shop. A chill swept across her skin, and all her blood drained to her feet.

A bolt of alarm shot through Dylan as he took

in Alaina's sudden pallor. He took her by the arm and guided her toward a chair. "Are you all right?"

Her heart was going about two ten. She stared at his hand on her forearm. His long, tan fingers were a stark contrast against her fair skin. The heat his touch generated flowed up her arm and across her chest, pooling behind her nipples.

Get hold of yourself, Alaina, she ordered sternly, stopping in her tracks. The only things she had in common with her mother, the oft-married Helene Barbach, were a few chromosomes and an allergy to shellfish. She herself wasn't at all the sort to succumb to common lust; she was much too in control of herself for that sort of idiotic nonsense.

"Princess?" Dylan asked again, a deep, genuine concern thrumming through him. "Are you all right?"

Alaina's head snapped up, her eyes glittering with temper. He was a threat, challenging her control with his damnable sexiness. The cad. She was as angry with him for being so darn attractive as she was at the situation his outrageous behavior had landed them in.

"Of course I'm not all right," she said crossly. "I'm being arrested."

Dylan plopped down on a chair, looking morose. "You're right. We're being run in like a couple of common lowlifes. It's the end of the world as we know it."

In an instant he was on his knees in front of Deputy Skreawupp's desk, his long scarf dusting the floor, his arms outstretched in a gesture of supplication. "Please, Deputy, you can't send me up the river to the big house! I couldn't make it, I tell ya!"

Alaina pressed a fist to her mouth to stifle her laughter. The man was outrageous. No matter how hard she tried to stay angry with him, he kept appealing to her sense of humor—with smashing success.

Dylan shot her a disgruntled look over his shoulder. "Could you hold the laughs? You're spoiling my big scene."

"Sorry," she mumbled, biting her lip.

He turned back to the deputy, instantly falling back into character. "I'd be a total wash in prison. I can't play the harmonica, and I don't know all the words to 'Nobody Knows the Trouble I've Seen.' "

"Jeez," the deputy grumbled, "what a weirdo."

"Actually, I'm a Time Lord," Dylan said, standing and dusting off the knees of his baggy trousers. "Dr. Who."

"Who?"

Alaina groaned and pressed a hand to her forehead. "Here we go again."

"Don't start with me, pal," the deputy said, shaking a meaty finger at Dylan. He narrowed his beady eyes until they were mere slits in his fleshy face. "I'll bust you like a ripe melon."

Dylan grimaced. "You have a real talent for visual imagery. Have you ever thought of writing children's books?"

A ferocious scowl was his only answer.

Dylan tugged down the bottom of his waistcoat, clearing his throat as he prepared to launch into his explanation. "You see, it's this way, Deputy. I was on my way to a science fiction theme party, dressed as Dr. Who. Tom Baker's Dr. Who, to be precise. He's my personal favorite. Though I'm also quite fond of Peter Davison's portrayal of the doctor." At the deputy's growl of impatience he decided to skip the details and get on with the story. "Anyhow, I stopped to assist this lovely lady with her car, and a huge misunderstanding ensued."

"You know Jayne Jordan?" Alaina blurted out. Dylan nodded.

"I should have guessed," she mumbled. If there was an oddball within fifty miles—and there were plenty in northern California—Jayne knew him. If they happened to be single men, she usually tried to coerce Alaina into going out with them. Jayne, who was a widow, was a notorious matchmaker when it came to her friends. Alaina shuddered to think of what oddball might have been awaiting her at the party tonight. Getting arrested may have had its upside after all.

"You're a friend of Jayne's?" Dylan asked. He had already surmised as much, but her nod of confirmation still surprised him. Alaina Montgomery didn't strike him as being the type to hang out with someone of Jayne's . . . uniqueness.

"We went to college together."

"So what say we get this Jayne broad down

here to vouch for you?" Deputy Skreawupp suggested. He took a bottle of triple-strength aspirin out of a desk drawer and shook out half a handful.

Alaina perked up. "You're not going to throw me in the clink?"

"Lady, you're more trouble than you're worth. I don't need it," he said flatly. "I'll let you both off with a fine for creating a public nuisance."

Alaina opened her mouth to protest. Suddenly Dylan was beside her, clamping a hand over her denial. Sliding down next to her, he smiled charmingly and whispered, "Quit while you're behind, Princess. So far, you've insulted his family name, called him incompetent, and threatened to sue. All in all, I'd say we're getting off lucky."

She sat back in her chair and absently rubbed her hand over her chin where Dylan had touched her. Calling Jayne in wasn't necessarily a great idea. Who knew what she would come in dressed up as? On the other hand, there really wasn't anyone else she could call. Of the trio of friends who had moved to Anastasia, Faith was easy to get to know, and Jayne was the kind of person who befriended people on sight. Alaina tended to hold herself a little apart from people. Instinctively wary of relationships, she could count her close friends on her fingers. Consequently, she knew virtually no one in her new home.

Faith would have been the one to call. She radiated trustworthiness. Besides, her husband-to-be was a former top-notch Federal agent. Deputy Screwup would have melted under the power of Shane Callan's stare. But Faith had gone to Maine to meet Shane's family.

The only other person Alaina knew well at all in Anastasia was the woman who rented out the other half of her duplex, her new secretary, Marlene Desidarian. Having the secretary of her soon-to-open law practice come down essentially to bail her out of jail did not seem a prudent business strategy.

That left Jayne.

"Deal," she said, sending the stony-faced deputy a dazzling smile.

Dylan had watched her as she'd contemplated. He had practically heard the well-oiled wheels whirring in her brain as she considered strategies. A grudging admiration knotted with a sense of foreboding in his chest. He was attracted to Alaina Montgomery—big-time. The wallop her smile delivered confirmed it; it wasn't even directed at him, and still he felt reverberations clear to his toes.

He frowned as he sat back and squared one booted leg over the other. He was definitely going to have to watch his step here.

The call to Jayne was confusing to say the very least, but that was no surprise to Alaina. She only hoped her scatterbrained friend had understood the message. The theme music from *Star Trek* had been blaring in the background, making conversation virtually impossible. All she could do now was wait, she thought as she slid back down on her chair, carefully arranging her sinfully short skirt to cover the tops of her thighs.

Dylan sipped the herb tea Mrs. Fletcher had served them, wondering what he was doing hanging around. He had been sufficiently vouched for. He was free to go. But...His gaze strayed Alaina's way. She looked sort of forlorn now that the fight was over. She wasn't at all the kind of woman he wanted to spend his time with, and yet...

It was those legs, he thought, groaning inwardly as he watched her cross one lovely gam over the other.

"So, you and Jayne went to college together."

"Yes. Notre Dame, class of '77," Alaina said, gritting her teeth as she realized she'd just dated herself.

"Well, I know Jayne's story. How did you end up in Anastasia?"

Chasing rainbows, Alaina thought, a small, rueful smile canting her lips. Running from one dream in search of another. Those weren't the answers she gave, however. Admitting confusion was tantamount to admitting a weakness. That wasn't something she did easily.

She gave Dylan a careless shrug. "I was burned out. I needed a change of scenery."

So, she would be here only temporarily, Dylan decided. She'd said she was the youngest partner in the history of her firm back in Chicago. That meant she had ambition. Ambitious women didn't stay long in a town like Anastasia. They came for the sea air and a dose of simplicity and quaint coastal charm, then they packed their Gucci bags and climbed in their yuppie-mobiles and headed back to their corporate offices for another round of ladder-climbing.

A sigh escaped him as his baser male instincts began mourning the departure of those mouth-watering legs.

She was going to be here only as long as it took her to recharge her ambition and work up a new appetite for conquering the male-dominated world. That made her less dangerous to him, didn't it? He knew she was all wrong for him, knew she wasn't staying. With those lines of distinction drawn, didn't that mean he could enjoy her company while she was here?

It was truly remarkable the rationalization a great pair of legs could inspire, he thought. He was actually contemplating spending time with Alaina Montgomery. The idea settled in his mind, then drifted lower as he imagined all the ways he could enjoy those beautifully shaped limbs that were now encased in black mesh stockings. Let's see, there was looking, caressing, wrapping them around his—

"What does one do at a bar and bait shop?" Alaina queried, more to get his attention off her legs than anything. The intensity of his dark gaze had her squirming on her chair. Of course, she pretended not to be affected in the least. Why, her hands barely shook at all as she lit her cigarette. It was a real victory of a woman's higher nature over her animal instincts.

Dylan sent her a devilish smile, knowing full well women like Alaina had an innate disdain for men who didn't wear Brooks Brothers suits. A bar and bait shop was way out of the realm of respectability for her. He wondered cynically how bored she would have sounded had he informed her that he had once been a hotshot investment counselor. "I sell bait to sport fishermen, a buddy of mine rents them boats, then when they get back at the end of the day, they get drunk on my liquor and lie about all the big fish that got away."

She sent a thin blue stream of smoke into the air and arched a brow. "Sounds like a racket."

"Yeah. It's called free enterprise. Have dinner with me tomorrow night."

"I beg your pardon?" Alaina sat back in her chair, completely caught off balance by his request. What a devious tactic, changing subjects that way. She couldn't help but admire his strategy. He was handsome *and* clever. That was a rare and dangerously appealing combination.

"Dinner," he said affably. "You know, it's that meal at the end of the day."

She shot him a look. "I know what dinner is."

"Good, then we're over that hurdle." He leaned forward on his chair, warming to the idea of a date almost as much as he was warming up from leering at the lawyer's lovely legs. "I know a great little place up near Russian Gulch, very quiet, out of the way, great dance band. So, it's a date?"

"It's not a date!" Alaina declared, scooting over on her chair as if she were afraid to have him breathe on her. In fact, she was trying to escape the lure of his body heat and the shiver of delicious anticipation his suggestion had set loose inside her. She would not succumb to her hormones, she stated inwardly, though less emphatically than before. Her shoulders squared defensively, thrusting her full breasts out in a way that made Dylan groan low in his throat. "I won't go out with you. I hardly know you. Why, not an hour ago I thought you were a social deviant."

He looked wounded, dramatically clutching his hands to his heart as if her words had been a dagger plunged into his chest. "How can you say you hardly know me? How can you say that after all we've shared? We've been arrested together!" Leaning so close to Alaina, just a deep breath away from kissing her, he lowered his voice to a devastatingly sexy pitch. "We've shared handcuffs. I usually save that for the third or fourth date."

Ignoring the warm tingles his nearness—not to mention his audacious admission—brought on, Alaina gave him an incredulous look and shoved him back into his own space. "You're completely irreverent!"

"That's true. I don't have a reverent bone in my body. It made headlines in the *Enquirer* when

I was born: 'Mystery Baby Born Without Reverent Bones—Space Alien or Love Child of Elvis' Ghost?' "

"See there?" Alaina said, waving an elegant hand in a dismissive gesture as she bit back her laughter. Her cool blue eyes sparkled like ice on a sunny winter day. "I don't date men who read the *Enquirer*, let alone men who make the front page."

"Snob," he accused good-naturedly.

She smiled and tapped her ash into the cheap tin Reno, Nevada, souvenir ashtray she'd taken off Deputy Skreawupp's desk. "Yes, I am."

"And darn proud of it," Dylan declared emphatically, slapping his thigh.

"Naturally."

Dylan grinned. The impact of that dazzling smile nearly knocked Alaina off her chair. Lord, he was handsome, bar and bait shop or not. And he was really quite charming in a tacky sort of way.

"If you're going to do something, do it well, I say. Or, as my father likes to put it, if you go hunting for bear, don't come home with a greasy dead possum."

Alaina grimaced. "What a disgusting back-woods maxim."

"I come from disgusting backwoods stock," Dylan admitted with a smile. "Hayseeds and bumpkins abound on my family tree. We even have a mountain man or two."

"Better than I had imagined," Alaina quipped. "Still, it's another perfectly legitimate reason why I can't go out with you; you're ill-bred."

She was cut from the same cloth as Veronica Howard, all right, Dylan thought. But there was one big difference between Alaina Montgomery and his ex-wife. Alaina's sardonic tone was laced with martini-dry good humor. When Veronica had derided his background, she'd meant every word. Alaina seemed to enjoy playing the role of the upwardly mobile, materialistic ice princess, but he sensed there was more to her than that.

Catching a glimpse of her cleavage, he held his breath tight in his lungs. Brother, was there more to her!

"Do you have any illegitimate reasons for not going out with me?" he asked, his dark eyes gleaming with mischief.

"No, but I do have an illiberal thought or two."

"How about illicit thoughts?" He waggled his eyebrows, a smile tugging at his lips as he caught the light of amusement in her eyes. Pretty eyes, mesmerizing and translucent with a bit of an exotic slant to them. A man could get lost staring into those eyes. At the moment he couldn't help but think that wasn't such a bad idea.

Alaina stuck her patrician nose in the air and sniffed. "In your dreams, Harrison."

He cast a longing glance at her legs and muttered, "You've got that right."

She didn't fight her smile this time. Her lush mouth hitched up on the right, and she shook her head. The man might have been a complete buffoon, but she was having fun bantering with him. Clayton hadn't been much for verbal swordplay. Lies and deception, yes; he'd been a master at those. But when it came to the kind of sparring she was enjoying with Dylan Harrison, A. Clayton Collier had been a flop. He took things too literally and too seriously for double entendre.

Dylan Harrison, on the other hand, seemed to take nothing seriously. His attitude was rubbing off on her. Already she wasn't half as mad about getting arrested, though she did still feel betrayed by her car. And she didn't really feel all that nervous about turning into a clone of her mother. There wasn't a chance in hell of her becoming seriously involved with Dylan; they were far too different. All she was feeling toward him now was chemistry. It was possible to feel chemistry and still be in control, she decided. He was a handsome man, and charming in a bizarre, Bill Murray sort of way. What woman wouldn't respond to that on a basic level?

Still, she decided, it was probably best to set him straight right off. "I'm not looking for a relationship," she announced, giving him her most serious courtroom expression.

"That makes two of us," Dylan admitted. "All I want is a dinner companion and a dancing partner. People tend to stare when I go dancing by myself."

"I can imagine."

"So, you want to know more about me?"

"Not really," she lied smoothly.

Dylan pressed on as if she had begged him to

continue. "I don't really like to talk about myself, but if you insist. My name is Dylan Henry Harrison. I'm forty years old as of ten twenty-two this evening. I like to sail and play the baritone. My favorite color is fuchsia, and I have long, bony feet, but I'm not vain about them in the least. What time should I pick you up?"

"Fuchsia?"

"Yes." He leaned toward her again, a sexy smile turning his lips and lighting dark fires in his coffee-brown eyes. "You'd look great in fuchsia," he confided in a low, pillow-talk whisper. On impulse he lifted a finger to trace the clean line of her jaw. Her skin was like silk, cool and soft. "You'd look great out of fuchsia too. So what time—"

A horrified look came over his face as he sat up, his back ramrod straight. "Oh, damn. Time. What time is it?" He grabbed Alaina's wrist and consulted the slim gold Rolex she wore, then bolted out of his chair, grabbed up the receiver of Deputy Skreawupp's phone, and start punching buttons, muttering curses under his breath.

Alaina watched him, only slightly bemused.

She had already decided that nothing the man could do would surprise her.

"Hello, Cori, sweetheart? It's Daddy."

Except that.

Alaina braced a fist under her chin to keep her jaw from dropping and putting a dent in her chest. Unfortunately, there was nothing she could do to keep her heart from dropping into her stomach and sinking like a scuttled ship. A wave of nausea swept over her, leaving her feeling clammy and cold and looking for the ladies' room.

He was married. He was a daddy. He was a philandering lothario, a licentious libertine. And she had been about to agree to have dinner with him! Only to humor him, of course. It wasn't that she was truly all *that* attracted to him or anything, she insisted, disregarding the wild humming of her hormones as she stared at him.

Wasn't looking for a relationship, indeed! No wonder. He already had a relationship, complete with little relationships attached! A nice, quiet, out-of-the-way restaurant. Right. So none of his in-laws could stumble across him!

Anger swirled through her in a whirlwind,

mixing with another emotion, one she couldn't quite define. It was sort of like disappointment intermingled with guilt. She did her level best to ignore it and concentrate on fury instead. Fury was pure and uncomplicated and it hurt a hell of a lot less.

Suddenly the front door burst open, and Jayne Jordan made a grand entrance. She was dressed as some kind of fairy, complete with gossamer wings and a sparkling wand. Layers of white chiffon floated over her petite form like a cloud. Her dark auburn hair was alight with silver and gold glitter. Right behind her was an enormous hairy creature who had to duck to get through the door. Once inside, he took his head off—or rather, his mask— and looked around, a pleasant grin revealing a space between his two front teeth.

"Jeepers criminy," Deputy Skreawupp muttered in utter disgust as he rose from his desk and moved to stand in front of it with his arms crossed above his potbelly. "Bunch of demented communists."

"Alaina!" Jayne exclaimed, her dark eyes wide with worry and wonder. She hurried through the little gate and rushed back to her friend, her wand bobbing. "Honey, are you all right? What happened?"

"A slight misunderstanding," Alaina said tightly, forcing herself to her feet and willing her knees to support her weight. She deliberately avoided looking Dylan's way, riveting her icy stare on her friend instead. "First, let me say just briefly that, were I a vindictive sort of person, I would make your life a living hell for insisting I wear this costume. Since I love you like a sister, I'll forgive you."

Jayne had the grace to look contrite, though she didn't apologize.

"There was a minor incident with my car, and Deputy Screw—*Skreawupp* came to the erroneous conclusion that I was a—er—"

"Hooker," the deputy said with a grunt.

Alaina shot him a venomous look. "Thank you *so* much."

Jayne burst into laughter. She turned to the deputy. "Oh, honey, you couldn't get much further from the truth. She's Princess Andora of the

Zanatares, upholder of the Sacred Laws of the Seventh Galaxy in the ninth millennium."

The deputy's beetle brows rose and fell like a pair of dancing woolly caterpillars. "And who are you? Tinker Bell?"

"No," Jayne drawled with an impish smile. "I'm Sarafina, high priestess of the fairies of the primordial forests of Mandrocona." She gestured toward the hairy mountain standing behind her. "My friend Arnie is a Wookie. You know, like Chewbacca in *Star Wars*."

Arnie tucked his fake head under his arm and nodded at the deputy. "Ya, pleased to meet you," he said in a heavy Austrian accent.

"Jayne," Alaina said through her teeth, "you're not exactly helping my cause here. Vouch for me. As a human film critic from twentieth-century Earth."

The formalities were dispensed with quickly. Deputy Skreawupp seemed as eager to be rid of Alaina as Alaina was eager to get out of the jail— and out of Dylan Harrison's tainted company. The instant the deputy told her she was free to go, she turned on her glittery spike heel and marched for the door.

"What about Dylan?" Jayne asked, hesitating at the gate. She exchanged an odd look of concern with Arnie the Austrian Wookie.

Behind them, Dylan pressed the telephone receiver to his shoulder. His questioning gaze captured Alaina's as she paused with her hand on the brass doorknob. "What time should I pick you up for dinner?"

"When hell freezes over!" she shouted, simply unable to restrain her temper another second.

Dylan frowned. "They only serve until ten."

Why? Why were men such bastards? Not that it mattered to her personally, Alaina told herself. Not a bit. Not anymore. She was all through looking for the elusive Mr. Right. How long had her mother been on the hunt for him? Helene had gone through five husbands and who knew how many near-misters, and she was still looking. It was pointless. One had better odds of finding the

Holy Grail while on a tour of the Chicago sewer system.

Alaina sipped her Scotch and stared out the bay window. She was curled up on the window seat, wrapped in her gray silk dressing gown. Across from her, illuminated only by moonlight pouring in through the sheer curtains, was Julia, the petite black cat who had come with the duplex. Alaina had never been much for cats, but Julia, a very snobby superior feline, had simply ignored Alaina's attempts to remove her from the house. Now she sat on the velvet cushion, meticulously cleaning her dainty paws, ignoring Alaina completely. Not to be outdone, Alaina ignored her right back.

Men were bastards because that was the way of the world. People were essentially selfish and greedy. Alaina had learned early on that the soundest philosophy a person could have was to look out for oneself, because nobody else gave a damn. Over the years she had found few exceptions to the rule.

Her friend Bryan had always frowned at her cynical analysis of the human race. Faith had been sympathetic. Faith was always sympathetic; it was one of her most endearing qualities. Jayne had told her she didn't know where the center of the Earth was. Jayne was such a flake.

Alaina had moved to Anastasia in part to be with her friends. They were the closest she had ever—or would ever—come to having a family. She was an only child, one who had not been planned for or welcomed into her parents' lives. With Faith, Jayne, and Bryan, she had found a sense of belonging, a home for a heart that was far more fragile than she would ever let on.

Twelve years had passed since the Fearsome Foursome had first dreamed up the plan to move to this picture-postcard town on California's northern coast. From the crossroads of their graduation they had all rushed off in different directions in pursuit of the perfect future. They had chased their rainbows, and what had they found at the end of them? Three of them had found disappointment in one form or another. Only Bryan was still off on the chase, traveling the world as a psychic investigator.

A long sigh escaped Alaina as she ran a hand

back through her dark hair and tilted her head back against the window frame. It was time to start over, time to put past disillusionments behind her and get her life back into tidy little compartments, the way she liked it. She was by nature a perfectionist, neat and analytical. That was the only sensible approach to life. Emotional entanglements were messy and painful as a rule, so she generally avoided them.

She had her small circle of friends. She had a nice home impeccably decorated with tasteful art deco–style furniture. She had financial security, which was basically the only kind of security she'd ever had. And soon she would have her own law practice, where she could follow her own code of ethics and choose her own clients. It was practically the ideal existence.

She was absolutely *not* looking for a relationship.

But as she stared out into the night and secretly acknowledged the too familiar pang of loneliness in her heart, she thought it might have been nice to go dancing.

Chapter 3

"Marlene, I really don't see the need for this line 'Astrological Sign' on the client information form," Alaina said, congratulating herself on her patience. She put the form back on the stack on her secretary's desk, crossed her arms over her blue silk designer T-shirt, and calmly awaited a comment from the woman.

Marlene Desidarian paused in her task of driving a nail in the wall behind her desk to shoot her boss a look. "You'll thank me for it," she said in a voice that made Roseanne Barr sound like a songbird. "Well be able to tell at a glance how compatible they're going to be with your personality."

"All I really need to know is whether or not I'm interested in their case, and whether or not they can pay me."

"Capricorns," Marlene muttered disparagingly as she turned and gave the nail a good thump.

Compromise, Alaina knew, was an unpleasant but necessary fact of life. It was a word she despised but lived with. Sometimes a person simply had to trade off one priority to achieve another. Marlene Desidarian was a living example of this law at work in her life.

Marlene might have been fifty or she might have been sixty. It was difficult to tell, and she was creatively evasive when questioned about it—a skill Alaina herself cultivated, so she let the issue slide. Marlene was tall and built like a side-by-side refrigerator. Her fading silver-blond hair fell down her back in a long, utilitarian braid, and she dressed like a hippy. She was an enthusiastic student of astrology and mythology and auras and karmas and all of the same goofy mystical California nonsense Jayne Jordan was into.

For these reasons Alaina would ordinarily have avoided Marlene, but Marlene could also type a hundred and ten words a minute, and she had a forbidding look that could stop an office supplies salesman in his tracks at twenty yards.

Oh, hell, Alaina admitted to herself as she watched her secretary hang a perfectly horrid painting, she liked Marlene. The woman was undeniably weird, but she had a good heart. They had struck up an odd, argumentative sort of friendship practically the moment they'd met when Alaina had been inspecting the duplex as a prospective buyer.

"Marlene, you are not hanging that atrocious thing in here," she declared, planting her hands on her hips. She glared at the painting, which appeared to be an abstract of a woman with nine eyes and three breasts.

Marlene gave her a shrewd look. "What do you think it looks like?"

Instantly wary, Alaina held her true impression and said noncommittally, "It looks like an inkblot."

"It *is* an inkblot. You catch on fast for a lawyer."

Alaina ignored the insult. She waved a regal

hand at the splotch of blue on white. "It's coming down. I won't have prospective clients subjected to a Rorschach test the second they come into the office."

Shrugging tiredly, Marlene heaved a much-put-upon sigh, her broad shoulders sagging. She shook her head and tugged up one shoulder of her huge, purple, tie-dyed T-shirt. "If you say so, but you're missing the boat on a slick screening process."

"And you're missing the boat altogether," Alaina muttered under her breath as she turned to go into her private office to sort through her law books.

The suite she had rented consisted of three rooms and was located in a small, relatively new professional building just off Anastasia's main street. She looked around at the pristine white walls where her diplomas would hang, at the freshly laid gray carpet, at the two large windows that let the warm fall sunlight stream in through textured vertical blinds, and a proud, satisfied smile turned her lips. She had her much-coveted corner office, and she wasn't going to have to sell her soul for it.

This was going to be *her* practice. Alaina N. Montgomery, attorney at law. There were no senior partners to pay homage to. There were no duel-to-the-death, winner-take-all divorce cases, no trumped-up personal injury cases, no let's-make-the-kid-a-wishbone custody cases. There were no clients either, but that was only a temporary condition, a minor detail she wasn't concerned about in the least. She had ample confidence in her own abilities, and ample funds in her bank account to keep her going until she built up a clientele. The important thing was, she would be her own boss.

It wasn't that practices had been unethical at Abercrombie, Turtletaub, and Flinch. The firm was one of the most prestigious, highly respected in the Chicago area. And heaven knew, Alaina had taken to their aggressive style of law like a shark to water. It was just that within the last year or so she had begun suffering from a strange sort of dissatisfaction with her lot in life. One day she'd realized she had everything she'd wanted—

money, prestige, a certain amount of power—but she wasn't happy, and she didn't know why. And then, of course, there'd been that unpleasant business with Clayton.

She frowned, her hand absently stroking the spine of a leather-bound tome on jurisprudence. Odd, but she couldn't quite remember what A. Clayton Collier looked like. She could remember too clearly what his wife had looked like the fateful day she'd come to call. She remembered every detail of Mrs. Collier, right down to her red snakeskin pumps and matching handbag. But when she tried to call a man's face to mind, it was Dylan Harrison's she saw with his unruly hair and devilish grin.

Even though she'd met him only once and that had been nearly a week ago, she could remember his handsome features with alarming clarity. She remembered everything about him, every word they had exchanged, every glance, every arc of awareness that had passed between them.

Giving herself a mental shake, she began sorting through her books. The man had a wife and child and no scruples whatsoever. That was a combination she had learned to avoid. And if his marital status weren't enough to dissuade her from thinking about him, he ran a bar and bait shop, for Pete's sake. What on earth would she have in common with a man who sold swill and chum? Nothing.

Then why did she keep thinking about him? Why did she keep thinking of the way he'd traced his finger along her jaw? And why did she keep reliving that instant when he'd held her against the side of her car, his sexy mouth just a heartbeat from hers? Even when she'd suspected he was a lunatic, she'd been attracted to him.

A chill swept over her as she had a horrid thought. She suddenly envisioned Mrs. Dylan Harrison chasing her around her office wielding a giant fishhook.

Alaina swore through her teeth as she forcibly dismissed the image and returned her attention to her task.

"You're coming to dinner tonight." The announcement made from the door of her office was a statement of fact, not a question.

Alaina looked up at her secretary and frowned.

Ever since she'd moved into the duplex, Marlene had been trying to fix her up with a seemingly endless parade of eligible men. The woman was worse than Jayne when it came to matchmaking and utterly shameless in her efforts. It was embarrassing to say the very least. Alaina kept promising herself she would refuse the next time, but for some unfathomable reason, she had a hard time telling Marlene no.

This time was no exception. She sighed up into her stylishly cut bangs and tucked a strand of chestnut hair behind her right ear. "Promise me this isn't another blind date."

Marlene scowled, an expression that gave her an alarming resemblance to Deputy Skreawupp. She wouldn't quite look her boss in the eye. "It's a dinner party," she said flatly.

"Swear it."

"I swear it's a dinner party."

"A cleverly evasive answer if ever I've heard one. And believe me, I've heard zillions."

Going on the offensive, Marlene shook a finger at Alaina. A quartet of silver and turquoise bracelets rattled on her thick wrist. "You're too suspicious for your own good. What's the matter with you, thinking I'd stoop to trapping you into a blind date?"

"Oh, I don't know," Alaina said, her arms sailing upward in an exaggerated shrug. "Maybe the fact that you advertise in the yellow pages under 'Matchmakers.' "

"A person's got to make a living."

"Not at the expense of my social life. After last week's fiasco, I ought to turn you down flat." She shuddered at the memory and made a face. "I ought to sue you for emotional—not to mention sartorial—suffering."

"What? You didn't like Quenton Stockley?" Marlene's expression clearly indicated her incredulity at the prospect.

Alaina still marveled at the fact that she'd agreed to go out with the man. Marlene had shown up at her door one evening, unannounced, with Quenton in tow. Quenton Stockley was an anemic little man with terminal hay fever and what Alaina sincerely hoped was the last polyester leisure suit in the continental United States.

It was all Dylan Harrison's fault she had sacrificed an evening of her free time to Quenton Stockley. She had gone out with him only to escape her constant disconcerting thoughts of Dylan the dastardly philanderer.

Marlene propped a meaty fist on her hip. "What was wrong with Quenton?"

The list was endless. Alaina decided to choose one major fault and leave the rest. "He took me to a Three Stooges movie festival."

"So?"

"Grown men poking each other in the eyes is not my idea of cinema."

Marlene made a face and waved a beringed hand at her. "You're too fussy."

"I'm tastefully discriminating," Alaina corrected. "And for the billionth time, Marlene, I am *not* looking for a man. Please get that through your thick head."

A determined look on her face, the secretary stepped closer, trapping Alaina against the side of the table that was temporarily serving duty as a desk. She closed her eyes with a dramatic fluttering of her lashes and began running her hands all around Alaina's head and shoulders, not quite touching her.

"Jeez, Marlene, stop it," Alaina whined, cringing. "You know I hate when you do that."

The woman stepped back, shaking her head reproachfully. "Your aura is all out of whack."

"Small wonder," Alaina mumbled, turning back to her books, "what with you attacking me every time I turn around."

"A woman your age ought to have a man in her life," Marlene announced.

"What for? I can take out my own garbage," Alaina quipped. Her dark brows suddenly snapped down low over her eyes and turned to bore a look into her secretary's retreating broad back. "What do you mean—a woman my age?"

"Dinner's at seven."

"Okay, guys, I'm leaving now!" Dylan called, hastily checking his appearance in the dusty mirror that hung above the cluttered table in the front entry. He ran a hand back through his unruly hair and gave his hand-painted leather tie a jerk to set it straight, then he turned to say good-bye to his children.

Nine-year-old Sam stood there with an exact-scale replica of the starship *Enterprise* cradled in his arms. He had his mother's sandy hair and his father's lanky frame and an expression that was far too mature for his age. "You appear magnetically prepossessing this evening, Dad."

Dylan blinked, a little taken aback as he always was by his son's rather adult intellect. "You've been reading the thesaurus again. Do you like my tie?"

"It's awesome," Sam said seriously.

"Thanks." Dylan dug through the rubble on the table for his car keys as he spoke. "I won't be late, but you guys will be in bed by the time I get home, so I'll call by eight-thirty."

The Harrison children exchanged a significant look. As usual, Sam acted as spokesman. "You'll tuck Cori in when you get home, won't you?"

Dylan hunkered down in front of his little girl, a tender smile turning his lips. "I wouldn't miss it."

Cori leaned against the family dog, Scottie, an

enormous shaggy beast of indiscriminate background. The little girl's brown eyes stared up owlishly at her father. Dylan's heart clenched in his chest.

He had been hurt when Veronica had divorced him and moved to L.A. to pursue her career, but his deepest pain came from the knowledge that what had happened between himself and his wife had left lasting scars on their children. Sometimes he thought he'd never forgive himself or Veronica for that. What they'd done to each other had been the choice of consenting adults; their children had been innocent casualties in the war.

Sam had somehow seen the need to grow up overnight. Bypassing the rowdy, carefree phase of childhood, he was a quiet, meticulous, studious adult in the body of a nine-year-old boy. He spent much of his free time in academic pursuits or working with their extensive collection of science fiction memorabilia rather than with friends. And he had grown fiercely protective of Cori, seemingly determined to fend off any threat of hurt to his little sister.

Cori, who had been only five at the time of the

breakup, had reacted by retreating into herself. She was too young to understand or deal with her emotions regarding her mother's departure from the family, Dylan doted on her—on both children, really, but on Cori in particular—doing his level best to make her feel safe and secure in his love. But even now, nearly two years after the divorce, Cori rarely spoke unless asked a direct question that couldn't be answered by a nod or a shake of her head.

Dylan hooked a finger under his daughter's chin and tilted her face up to plant a kiss on her cheek. "No wild parties while I'm gone. Mind Mrs. Pepoon." He wrapped his arms around her and gave her a hug. "I love you."

"Love you, Daddy," Cori murmured, bussing his cheek.

Reluctantly pulling back, Dylan reached up and ruffled Sam's sandy hair. Standing, he gave a proper Federation salute to his son. "Mr. Spock, you have the con."

"Aye aye, Captain. I hope you have an enjoyable repast."

Dylan shook his head. "I'm sure I will. Why don't you watch some TV tonight?"

Sam gave him a quizzical look, wrinkling his freckled nose.

"See you later, Mrs. Pepoon!" Dylan called to his housekeeper.

Taking one last glimpse in the mirror, he was gone.

He was not looking forward to this evening. Marlene Desidarian had been hounding him for weeks to come to dinner, and he had managed to put her off, but she was a friend and he'd known he couldn't delay the inevitable forever.

Marlene had doggedly been struggling to marry him off ever since they'd met when he'd first moved to Anastasia after the divorce. No matter how many times he told her he wasn't interested in trying matrimony a second time around, she persisted.

The entire situation left him feeling vaguely queasy. After the breakup of his marriage to Veronica he was understandably wary of making a commitment—not only for the sake of his own heart, but for the sake of his children as well. What if a second marriage didn't work any better than the first? It would kill him to put Cori and Sam through that kind of hell again. On the other hand, he harbored a genuine fear that his children were being cheated. He worked very hard at being a good father, but maybe his kids needed a mother too.

Well, he sighed as he pulled his Bronco up along the curb in front of Marlene's duplex, maybe someday he would find a woman he could feel safe marrying. She would be a far cry from Veronica, that was for sure. No more ambitious career women for him. He had thrown off the trappings of the yuppie lifestyle in favor of a saner existence. Next time—if there was a next time— he would find a woman so domestic, she'd make Donna Reed look bad. In the meantime...

He steeled his resolve and looked up at the neatly painted Victorian house, cream with blue trim, bulging with bay windows that gleamed amber in the fading light of dusk. He was ready. He could take anything Marlene the matchmaker would throw at him this evening.

* * *

Alaina Montgomery. Those legs couldn't possibly belong to any other woman. Dylan's heart slammed into his ribs as his gaze slid down from a shapely derriere decked out in a snug, well-cut gray skirt to the backs of two elegant knees and a pair of calves that made his palms break out in a sweat. His fingers twitched to trace down the length of the silk stockings that housed those gorgeous limbs. Shapely calves tapered to slender ankles that led to feet encased in Italian leather pumps.

Lord, he'd dreamed about those legs. He'd taken cold showers because of those legs. This past week all he'd seen upon closing his eyes were those legs. The woman attached to them was all wrong for him, of course, but those legs . . .

They were alone in Marlene's dining room. Dylan had let himself in, hoping to have a chance to scope out the situation before Marlene started throwing single women at him. Alaina was bent over the service bar that connected the dining room and the kitchen, reaching for a bread basket.

Dylan strolled up behind her, his hands stuffed into the pockets of his baggy chinos to keep from touching her. He had an almost overwhelming urge to goose her and wondered if it would be worth getting belted for. Probably, he decided, eyeing her fanny, but he managed to restrain himself just the same.

"Fancy meeting you here, Princess," he said, leaning closer than was strictly prudent and catching a whiff of very expensive perfume. "I take it you're on Marlene's hit list too."

Alaina wheeled at the sound of his clear, resonant baritone, her blue eyes wide as her heart went into a frantic dance. Her fingers went suddenly numb and she dropped the basket she held. Dinner rolls leaped out and bounced all over the floor.

"You!" she said with a gasp, her stunned gaze taking in his appearance in one swift glance. The man didn't have an ounce of good taste. He wore rumpled tan chinos, high-top sneakers, a wildly printed Hawaiian shirt, and a skinny leather necktie with a hula dancer painted on it. "What are *you* doing here?"

Dylan frowned down at the bouncing buns. "Having dinner, provided you don't throw too much of it on the floor."

"Marlene invited *you*?" she asked, incredulous and horrified. In spite of his awful outfit, she was well aware of just how good-looking Dylan Harrison was and just how he affected her unmanageable feminine instincts. She had hoped to avoid temptation by avoiding him. It certainly wasn't her idea of a good time to be constantly reminded she was wildly attracted to a married man who ran a waterfront beer joint.

"Yes." Dylan grinned, flashing his even white teeth at her. "I'm on a lot of people's A-list. Hard to believe, isn't it?"

Alaina's slim nose lifted a notch as she caught a whiff of his atrocious aftershave. "Virtually impossible. Why would Marlene invite you? You're married."

Dylan's straight brows leaped up his forehead. "Since when?"

"Ha!" Alaina exclaimed, summoning all the snootiness she possessed and wearing it like a shield. "Don't think you can pull the wool over my eyes!"

He gave her a lazy smile. "Can I pull it over some other choice part of you?"

"You can choke on it," she declared, her eyes narrowing as she regarded him in utter contempt. "I won't have anything to do with a married man."

"That makes two of us. Finally, we find we have something in common!"

"I heard you on the phone the other night."

Boy, she was cute when she was in a snit, he decided. Instead of being angry at her attack, he was actually kind of pleased. Wrong for him or not, he was glad to see her again. She was fun to fight with and wonderful to look at, and he couldn't help wondering how that sexy mouth of hers would taste. "Hearsay isn't admissible in a court of law."

"Neither is a punch in the nose, but that's what you're going to get if you try anything, buster." She brandished her fist in front of her to illustrate her point.

"My, you're feisty. I'm the one who should be

upset. You were eavesdropping on my private conversation."

Her index finger popped out of her fist and she poked Dylan on the chest with it. "So, you admit it then?"

"Admit what?"

"That you have children."

"Yes. Wholeheartedly. Enthusiastically. I have children."

"And a wife!" she declared, going for the full confession.

"Ex. I'm divorced."

Alaina's jaw dropped as the force of her offensive hit a brick wall. "Divorced?" she questioned dumbly.

"A concept I'm sure you've benefited from on more than one occasion," Dylan said with more than a hint of bitterness. After what he'd been through, he had no great love of lawyers—female or otherwise. "Divorce is a lucrative slice of the judicial pie, is it not, counselor?"

The wind thoroughly taken from her sails, Alaina sighed. "Yes, it is."

She felt like an utter fool, an unfamiliar and

distinctly unwelcome sensation. Why had it not occurred to her that he might be divorced? Half the men his age were divorced. She supposed she was just overly skittish of rogue husbands since Clayton. When she'd heard Dylan talking to his child over the phone, she had jumped to what for her was a natural, if unpleasant, conclusion.

So he wasn't married. *Hmmm.* A mysterious warmth swept through her at the thought. Dylan Harrison was unattached. That didn't change the fact that she wasn't interested in a relationship, she reminded herself rather halfheartedly. Nor did it change the fact that he was not at all her type. And the fact that he was not her type didn't change the fact that he had sexy, wavy, dark hair shot through with sun-kissed threads of blond and red or that his mouth looked as if it were made strictly for long, slow, deep kisses.

"Silent for a full twenty seconds," Dylan announced, consulting his watch. "That must be some kind of record. Should we be calling the people at Guinness?"

He grinned at Alaina, then his expression suddenly changed from one of teasing mischief to one of stunned disbelief as his gaze dropped to the bodice of her jewel-blue blouse. "Holy Hannah! It's the Crystal of Kalamari!"

His hands lifted toward her breasts, and Alaina jumped back against the service bar, her blood shooting through her veins. Dimly she wondered if there wasn't something drastically wrong with her, the way she seemed to become aroused every time this man behaved like a lunatic.

"I beg your pardon?" she asked, her husky alto voice nothing but a breathless whisper.

Managing to leash his excitement an instant before he laid his hands on her, Dylan curled his fingers into fists. He swallowed down a hard knot of air, his eyes still riveted to the piece of jewelry Alaina wore pinned just above her left breast. "That pin you're wearing," he said softly, as if he were afraid of being overheard, "may I ask how you came by it?"

Not daring to move, Alaina glanced down. The pin she wore had been a gift from Bryan Hennessy. It was an interesting little prism of glass cut in the shape of an inverted V. She wore it, she told herself, because it amused her and because it reminded her of a dear friend, not because of the rainbows trapped inside its clear walls. Bryan was the believer in rainbows, not she.

"It was a gift from a friend," she said, feeling as if she'd just been thrust into the middle of an Indiana Jones movie. "Does it have some significance?"

Dylan almost groaned aloud. Did an authentic Crystal of Kalamari pin have significance? As an avid collector of science fiction memorabilia, he had been searching for this piece for more than twenty years. What an odd bit of luck to find one pinned to the lush, ripe breast of Alaina Montgomery.

Lush, ripe breast, he mused, belatedly realizing that he once more had Alaina pinned up against an immovable object. Man, she had gorgeous breasts! He'd had his share of dreams about them as well as about her legs. The neckline of her blouse didn't afford him a view of her cleavage as her Princess Andora outfit had, but the fine silk still outlined the feminine mounds to perfection. In his imagination he already knew how they would feel in his hands—heavy and warm. And he would have bet his Space Marauders decoder ring that they were encased in a scandalously expensive, deliciously cut, sheer black French-lace bra.

She shifted against the counter, and the overhead light caught the crystal just right. The vivid colors of the rainbow within it drew Dylan's eye. It struck him that the pin was a very whimsical accessory for a woman who projected such a tough image. He lifted his gaze and tried to see past Alaina's cool barriers, a dozen questions stuck in his throat. He didn't ask any of them, but held his breath as a fine thread of awareness stretched between them like spun glass, fragile and tenuous.

"Dylan Harrison, when did you get here?" Marlene demanded to know as she powered open the swinging door between the kitchen and the dining room with a thrust of her hip. She held a steaming bowl in each hand. A flowing orchid caftan covered her ample form.

The spell was broken. Dylan stepped back from Alaina, casually tucking his hands into his pants pockets, hoping to disguise the fact that he was about half turned on from fantasizing about her underwear. "Hours ago, Marlene. You must have fallen into a time warp."

"I fell into ten pounds of mashed potatoes," she said, plunking the dishes down on the table. "I hope you're hungry."

"Oh . . . ," Dylan drawled, casting a wolfish look Alaina's way, "my mouth is literally watering."

Alaina smiled and rolled her eyes, wondering giddily when her heart was going to stop racing.

"Good." Marlene turned to face them. "I see you two have met."

"As you no doubt intended," Dylan said dryly.

"Actually, I wanted you to meet Ramona Madrone. She's in the den." She shrugged as she gave up the flimsy pretense of the innocent dinner party. Alaina's black scowl didn't faze her as she glanced at her boss. "And I wanted you to meet Morton Sternberg. He's in the den too." She looked from Alaina to Dylan, waving a hand between them as she frowned. "The two of you? You're not compatible in the least."

It was on the tip of Alaina's tongue to protest. Her hormones had their own idea of compatibility.

They could have lit up all of Anastasia with the electricity that zinged between herself and Dylan Harrison. But she bit her tongue on the admission and tucked her chin defensively, as if Marlene's charge of incompatibility were a terrible insult.

I'm losing my mind, she decided calmly as she went to stand behind a chair at the dinner table. Why she would want to be considered compatible with a lascivious, licentious lunatic was beyond her. The Crystal of Kalamari, indeed. She had to admit, though, it had been a creative way of getting within touching distance of her breasts. She had to give him points for his style, unorthodox as it was.

She refused to wonder about the moment that had passed between them. Awareness like that seemed a dangerous thing to contemplate. So did the wanting it stirred deep within her. Wanting meant vulnerability, vulnerability left a person open to hurt, and hurt was to be avoided at all cost. But...

She looked across the table just as Dylan glanced away. The hula girl tie made her shake her head in disbelief. There was something ridiculously tempting about him. It was damned annoying.

Their respective dinner partners turned out to be everything Marlene's blind dates usually were and then some. That the woman ever made a nickel as a matchmaker was a minor miracle. Alaina thought it was a wonder no one had ever threatened to sue.

Ramona Madrone was a prosthesis builder from Ukiah, thin as a whip with the overbite of a parrot. Morton Sternberg, as it turned out, was an orthodontist with a fake leg. If ever two people were compatible, it had to be Ramona and Morton.

The meal passed pleasantly enough, considering. Dylan kept the conversation rolling, orchestrating the topics so Ramona and Morton became thoroughly acquainted with each other. Alaina smiled to herself. So she wasn't the only one who thought the two made a dandy pair. Only Marlene seemed displeased with the idea, frowning and grumbling down at her mashed potatoes.

Alaina spent much of the dinner surreptitiously watching Dylan. He seemed to enjoy usurping Marlene's authority. And he was darn good at it, she admitted, unaccountably pleased by the fact that there was a sharp intellect lurking beneath that horrible outfit of his. Twice he caught her looking at him and shot her a wink and a smile, and she marveled at the wave of tingles that washed over her.

After the meal they all moved into Marlene's den, a room crammed with all sorts of mystical oddities. She had everything from astrological charts to an honest-to-goodness crystal ball. Dylan got Marlene off on what he knew would be a long-winded explanation of channeling, then discreetly slipped out the side door to the porch with Alaina in tow.

"That was rude," Alaina said affably. She settled back against the porch railing and reached into her small purse for a cigarette and her lighter.

"Why?" Dylan asked, frowning as he watched her light up. "We left her with a captive audience."

She exhaled a stream of blue into the night air, her eyes sparkling. "That's what I meant. Leaving

Ramona and Morton trapped like that. Marlene will go on with that malarkey for hours, and they're too polite to tell her to put a cork in it."

"I take it you don't believe in the magical, mystical—"

"—malarkey. No, I don't. I believe in jurisprudence, three-day weekends, and really good Scotch."

"Hmm, a cynic," Dylan murmured, his eye straying to the pin she wore. "Then you probably wouldn't have any sentimental objections to parting with that little glass bauble you're wearing—for the right price, of course."

"I would mind," she said, fingering the prism and finding it oddly warm to the touch. "It was a gift from a friend. I wouldn't dream of parting with it."

"A special friend?" he asked, pretending a casualness he didn't feel. He didn't like the idea of some other man having prior claim to Alaina's legs, not to mention the crystal. In fact, he felt downright possessive about it, which really wasn't like him at all.

"He's like a brother to me."

He just managed to swallow his sigh of relief. "Well, if you won't sell it, I suppose I could marry you. Then it would be mine by relation, so to speak."

Alaina cringed, though her heart gave a strange thump at his suggestion. "Please," she said, rolling her eyes, "don't mention that word to me."

" 'Marriage'?"

She winced.

"Not interested, huh?" He supposed he shouldn't have been surprised. Moreover, he shouldn't have been disappointed, but he was.

"It's nothing personal," she assured him. "Though, of course, you are, in fact, not my type. Having seen far more bad ones than good ones, I find marriage in general an unappealing prospect. Why should I bother trying it when I have a perfectly satisfactory life as it is?"

"A career, a great wardrobe, a BMW—what more could a yuppie girl ask for?" Dylan said sardonically as he leaned back against a post.

"Hey, I've got my life, you've got your bar and

bait shop. To each his own tastes," she said, casting a pointed look at his necktie. The hula girl glowed under the porch light.

"I guess," he conceded. "In point of fact, you're not my type either."

"How rude of you to say so." Alaina smiled to cover the fact that his statement rankled a bit.

"Can I help it you're not exactly June Cleaver?" Dylan shrugged. "Besides, I'm a rude, crude sort of guy—which brings me to my next proposition."

"I can hardly wait."

"Since *you're* not looking for a relationship and *I'm* not looking for a relationship, and Marlene is determined to bulldoze us into relationships, why don't we band together?"

Alaina eyed him skeptically. "Just what are you proposing?"

Dylan pressed on, warming to his impulsive stroke of brilliance. He was a genius. He could get off Marlene's *marry*-go-round and get Alaina's legs all to himself in one fell swoop. If he could spend some time with her, maybe he could talk her into parting with the crystal. And deeper down was the notion that, if he could spend some time with her, maybe he could show her that having it all didn't necessarily refer to imported cars and high-resolution television.

"Keeping company," he said. "We give the appearance of being involved in a loose but committed sort of relationship. It would be like our own private escort service. We'd go out with each other, keeping well-meaning matchmakers at bay."

"Keeping company," Alaina murmured, considering. It was an interesting theory. Lord knew she was sick to death of her friends trying to pair her off with men they thought would be perfect for her. And Dylan was fun to spar with. If she could get over the fact that he dressed with all the flare of a color-blind gypsy, it might be an interesting alliance at that.

She didn't allow herself to look any deeper into her reasons for considering his proposition. She told herself it didn't have anything to do with the moment that had passed between them in the dining room or the way he had touched her cheek the other night or the unexpected pang of gushy sentiment she'd felt when he had excused himself from the dinner table so he could call his kids and wish them sweet dreams.

"Interested?" he asked, studying her expression carefully as she thought.

"Maybe."

Dylan's heart beat a little quicker at the prospect of her accepting his offer. Her motives weren't important just now. The important thing was getting the opportunity. It would be up to him to make the most of it.

"I don't know about you, but I've got a couple of social events coming up where I will be considered fair game for all unfettered females. It sure would be nice to have a safe date that didn't have designs on my marital status."

Alaina nibbled one corner of her lush lower lip and turned to lean sideways against the porch railing and stare off into the night. She thought of the social events she had coming up—the Bar Association dinner dance, Faith's wedding. She thought of Morton Sternberg, who wore a foot-long strand of hair combed horizontally across his bald head, and Quenton Stockley of the leisure suit and Three Stooges film festival.

Keeping company with Dylan Harrison seemed like a concept with a lot of merit. They could definitely help each other out, she rationalized. And of course there was no danger of either of them getting in too deep; they were simply too different. Besides, they had both categorically stated they were not interested in a genuine relationship.

It could be kind of fun, she thought, absently brushing the knuckles of her right hand over the pin she wore. And maybe, she thought with a touch of wistfulness, maybe they could go dancing.

"What do you say, Princess? Rather take your chances with Morton the orthodontist?"

Alaina shrugged, slanting him a teasing and unconsciously flirtatious look that hit Dylan like a mortar. "I don't know. He did say I have a lovely bite."

"And you didn't slap his face? You shameless hussy."

She chuckled as she tapped out her cigarette on

the porch railing. Yes, this could be a lot of fun. She liked Dylan Harrison and he liked her. There was nothing dangerous in liking.

"You've got yourself a deal, Harrison," she said, offering her hand to him in a businesslike fashion.

He took it with a devilish grin and on impulse pulled her into his arms, bent her over backward, and planted his mouth on hers.

Chapter 4

You're in big trouble, Montgomery.

It was Alaina's one rational thought before she succumbed completely to the warm, wild taste of Dylan's mouth. She'd been right. That mouth of his was made for this—a long, slow, deep kiss. Taken by surprise, taken by a storm of sudden desire, she clung to his broad shoulders and let him sweep her senses away.

His mouth slanted across hers lazily, warming as she responded. The heat and taste of him was instantly addictive. She made a soft sound of surprise and surrender as she let him nuzzle her lips apart and allowed his tongue access to the honeyed heat beyond.

You've stuck your foot in it now, Harrison, Dylan thought as a brief but oppressive sense of impending doom descended on him. Well, not his foot precisely, but the implication was the same. He was in trouble. He hadn't meant to kiss her like this. He'd meant to give her a cocky, innocent smack on the mouth just to see the look on her face. But the instant lips had met lips something had gone very wrong.

Or was that very right?

Hell, he didn't know. All he knew at the moment was that she tasted like no other woman he'd ever kissed—warm and exotic and curiously sweet. And the way she felt in his arms was enough to make a man lose his mind.

"Have you lost your mind?!" It was the first thing, the only thing, Alaina could think to say when the kiss ended. She wasn't even certain if she was asking him or herself.

On wobbly legs she backed away from him, abruptly bumping into the porch railing. Her heart was racing like an Indy car. Her mouth felt as if it were on fire, and it wasn't the only part of her that was burning.

Dylan stared at her, looking astounded, though it was a toss-up as to whether his expression was for Alaina or for himself. His chest was heaving like a bellows. Holy Hannah, what had he just started?

"Um...that was an accident," he said for lack of a better explanation.

"Fender benders are accidents. Kisses do not fall under the heading of accident in my book," Alaina said, her temper rising.

Dylan scowled. "So sue me."

"Don't tempt me."

"Lawyers," he muttered. What had ever possessed him to make a deal with a lawyer? Temporary insanity caused by a pair of gorgeous gams. Damn, he was an idiot.

Blue eyes narrowed, Alaina fought the urge to scream. So he was above dealing with lawyers, was he? Brother. This from the owner of a bar and bait shop! It was just too galling. And kissing her had been so unpleasant, he had to call it an accident, huh?

"Take your deal and stick it, Harrison," she said through her gritted teeth. "I'd sooner keep company with a snake."

A strange sense of panic gave Dylan a boot as he watched her turn and storm for the door—not Marlene's door, but her own farther down the porch. He didn't want her to leave. It wasn't exactly a pleasant realization, but it was the truth.

He bolted after her, catching the edge of the door as she went inside and tried to swing it shut behind her. "Hey, wait. You can't renege. We made a deal. We shook on it. We kissed on it."

Alaina turned on one elegant heel and glared up at him, her hands knotted into fists at her sides. "That was an accident," she reminded him in an acid tone.

"Dammit, Alaina, a deal's a deal," he insisted as he followed her in.

"Did I sign anything?" she asked, her gaze casting about for something to throw at him that wasn't valuable. "Did you have a witness? Was there a notary present?"

He should have known better than to try to argue legality with an attorney; they could jump through loopholes like trick poodles through hoops. He was going to have to take a different tack if he was to salvage his flawed stroke of genius.

He prowled around Alaina's living room, taking in the impeccable state of it. It looked like something out of *House Beautiful*. Rose-colored overstuffed chairs and a sofa were artistically arranged on a rich carpet of silver gray. Waxy-white lilies stood in a black vase on a table along one wall. There wasn't so much as a dust mote out of place. It was immaculate, cool, classy, and perfectionistic—just like the woman who lived there.

He noticed idly that there were no personal mementos, no family photos, no hint as to who Alaina Montgomery really was. And it dawned on him for the second time that night that he wanted to know. The night they had been arrested he had suspected there was more to her than sassy bravado. When he'd kissed her, he'd caught a glimpse of something soft, something vulnerable within her. Something feminine and fragile that she kept hidden safe inside, guarding it with a shield of icy self-reliance. Unless he'd been imagining things, he had seen a flash of hurt flare briefly in her cool blue eyes when he'd stuck his foot in his mouth and called that kiss an accident.

Alaina watched him roam around the room. Wary, she stood near the sofa with her arms crossed in front of her. She should have been demanding he leave, but the words wouldn't form. She studied him instead. He moved with the lithe, unconscious grace of a dancer. He would have looked great in an Armani suit, the sharp, angular lines showing off his lanky, athletic frame. That image faded into one of him decked out in black tie, escorting her to the Bar Association dinner, sweeping her around the dance floor with a smile on his handsome face. Pain echoed through her like the sound of a gong at the thought that her image would never become a reality.

"I'm sorry I called the kiss an accident," Dylan said, stopping his pacing in front of her. "It wasn't an accident; it was a surprise."

That was a fact. It had surprised the hell out of him.

He arched a dark brow and shot Alaina a roguish little smile. "A pleasant surprise at that. I don't see that it's any reason to call off the deal."

In spite of her wariness, Alaina felt warmed by that little smile, and she answered it with one of her own. Her fears and anger evaporated like so much mist in the desert. "You're incorrigible."

"Utterly. However, that is not a crime."

"No," she agreed, reaching out to tug at the end of his hula dancer necktie. "This tie is a crime."

Dylan gave an exaggerated sigh, lifting his bold blade of a nose and rolling his eyes. "You have such a narrow vision of fashion."

"Yes, it's called taste," Alaina said, relaxing as she slipped off her pumps and padded across the carpet to the liquor cabinet. "Would you like a drink?"

"I don't suppose you have any Kool-Aid."

"I have Scotch."

"Pass," he said, slouching down on her sofa and propping his feet on the smoked-glass coffee table. "I don't drink."

"You own a bar."

"That doesn't mean I help myself to the inventory."

"Only the waitresses?"

"One of my two waitresses has a husband with no neck and arms like tree trunks. The guy makes Hulk Hogan look anorexic."

"And the other waitress?" she asked, casually batting his feet off her table as she passed.

"Is his identical twin sister, Chloe. And I do mean identical. She's got her eye on me, but I make it a policy never to date women who have more facial hair than I do." He sat ahead on the sofa and watched her settle in the chair across from him. "Speaking of dates, what do you say, Princess? Is the deal still on?"

Alaina looked down at her drink, swirling the amber liquid in the glass as she thought. She liked being with him. There wasn't anything wrong with that, was there? They could have some fun, have a few laughs. Where was the danger in that? She knew he wasn't looking for anything serious. Why that thought left her feeling hollow, she wasn't sure. She had stated more than once that she wasn't looking for a relationship either, hadn't she? Where was the harm in their spending time together?

"I guess," she murmured softly.

Dylan made no comment. He just sat back and looked at her, a strange warmth settling in his belly as if he were the one drinking the Scotch. A halo of lamplight fell on Alaina's brown hair, giving it a silvery cast. With her head bent down, her expression was an unguarded look of vulnerability. He knew she didn't realize it; she would never have let him see a weakness in her ice-princess armor. But he did see it, and it brought an odd feeling of tenderness to his heart.

Yes, he would spend time with Alaina. They would play this little game to fool their friends. But damned if he didn't suddenly want it to be a lot more than that.

"I should go," he said, checking his watch. "I promised my daughter I'd tuck her in. I don't want it to get too late."

"How old is she?" Alaina asked. She was genuinely curious about Dylan's children, but half her reason for asking was to keep him from leaving.

"Seven. The divorce was really hard on her. She can't understand why her mom went south in pursuit of fame and fortune. Little girls tend to think their mothers should want them."

That hit home. Alaina felt an instant kinship with Dylan's daughter. She frowned into her Scotch. "Some women aren't cut out to be mothers. Unfortunately, knowing that doesn't make it any easier to be their kid," she said candidly.

Dylan didn't comment. He knew instinctively Alaina did not make a habit of revealing that kind of personal information. He soaked it up like a sponge and craved more, but settled for what she'd given him.

"You have full custody?" she asked.

"Yes. Of Cori and my son, Sam, too. He's nine going on forty-two." He was curious how she would react to his kids and how his kids would react to her, but it seemed a dangerous train of thought to pursue, so he dismissed it. What he and Alaina were entering into didn't really allow for those kinds of questions . . . yet. He pushed himself to his feet and stretched lazily. "You'll meet them Sunday. At one of those dreaded social events I mentioned. How do you feel about picnics?"

"I'm game," she said as she stood and followed

him across the room. "Besides, a deal's a deal, right?"

He turned at the door and gave her a long look. "Right."

For an odd handful of seconds their gazes held, blue eyes and brown full of wary speculation about this threshold they were about to cross. Alaina glanced away first, dropping her gaze as Julia slipped in the door, wound her slender body around Dylan's ankles once, then trotted off in the direction of the kitchen.

"It's a magic crystal," Dylan said softly.

She looked up at him, puzzled.

"The Crystal of Kalamari. It's a magic crystal taken from the cave of the wizard Danathamien in *Tales of the Kalamari* by Frank D. Richard."

"My," she said, gazing down at the pin, at the rainbow of colors caught inside the prism of glass. "And all this time I thought it came from a flea market in the Sudan. Does it have any special powers?"

"Oh, yes," he said, much more serious in his answer than she had been in asking. "If your heart is pure and your desire is strong, the crystal can make your dreams come true."

Hooking a finger under her chin, he tilted her face up and dropped a kiss on her softly parted lips. "Good night, Princess. I'll see you on Sunday."

"So, you and Dylan hit it off, huh?"

It wasn't so much a statement as it was an exclamation of disbelief.

Alaina glanced up from her painting to shoot a disgruntled look Jayne's way. Jayne was seated cross-legged on the porch swing, head bent, painting her toenails orchid.

The Saturday-morning air was fresh and brimming with September sunshine. A small, round wicker table on the porch held a carafe of coffee and the remnants of the muffins Jayne had brought for breakfast. Alaina had been wondering how best to bring up the subject of Dylan Harrison. Jayne had taken the matter out of her hands.

"Is that so difficult to believe?"

"I'll say." Jayne dipped her brush back in the polish bottle and left it there so she could talk with her hands. "You two are from completely different planes of awareness. I know they say opposites attract, but honey, this is stretching it to the limit. I mean, Dylan is laid-back and easygoing, completely unconcerned about appearances and material possessions, and you're"—she hesitated, obviously searching for a diplomatic comparison—"not."

Alaina narrowed her eyes. She'd just about had it with people telling her how incompatible she and Dylan were. Marlene had been chanting it for two days like a mantra.

So she enjoyed the trappings of her success. Owning a BMW was hardly a serious character flaw. And so Dylan ran a bait shop and dressed like a street person. So what? He was witty and irreverent and fun.

Alaina stabbed her paintbrush in a glob of black on her palette and applied it to the canvas with aggressive strokes. Lord, was she actually defending him? Did it really matter what their

friends thought of their relationship? The important thing was that everyone know they were seeing each other. That was the whole idea, wasn't it?

An ill-tempered snarl simmered behind her
teeth. She glared at her canvas. She had been in on
the plan to fool everybody from the very start. It
wasn't as if the scheme had just hit her as a complete surprise. But now that she'd had a couple of
days to stew about it, the idea of "keeping company" had her feeling extremely crabby, and she
couldn't quite put her finger on why.

It was the ideal solution to the pervasive problem of mate-minded friends and their dubious
matchmaking skills. There was just something
about having Dylan Harrison considering her
"safe" that rubbed her the wrong way. The com-
petitor in her was chomping at the bit to prove
him wrong.

"So what have the two of you got planned?"

Alaina's paintbrush jerked upward, putting a
horn on her horse's head.

"Planned?" she asked, her heartbeat pounding.
Had Jayne seen through the ruse already? Impossible. Jayne didn't look for subterfuge, she looked

for symbolism. She snuck a look at her friend. "What makes you think we have something planned?"

"And you claim I don't make any sense," Jayne grumbled. She sat back, fanning her wet toenails with the loose tails of the oversize paisley shirt she wore above a flowing khaki skirt. "People who are seeing each other usually have things planned. You know, like dates."

"Oh. Dates. Of course." Alaina let out a measure of pent-up breath with each sentence. Her angular shoulders relaxed beneath the navy-blue polo shirt she wore. "I'm going with him to a picnic tomorrow."

Jayne looked impressed. Her dark eyes rounded even more than usual in her pixie face, the light of speculation gleaming deep within them. Alaina discounted it. It was just a picnic. Jayne was easily amazed. Grass growing amazed Jayne. "He's taking you to the bar and bait shop employee picnic? Hmm."

To fend off the advances of Chloe the bearded waitress. It was hardly a flattering thought. Nor was it a thought she could share with Jayne. Jayne and her penchant for matchmaking had gotten her into this situation in the first place.

"This sounds semiserious," Jayne said. She reached for a piece of blueberry muffin and nibbled on it thoughtfully. "So I guess I won't ask you if you want to go out with Knute Grabowski again."

Alaina's teeth went on edge. The name had roughly the same effect on her as fingernails on a chalkboard. "Promise me on pain of death you won't ask me to see Knute Grabowski again."

Knute was a lumberjack Jayne had met, God knew where, befriended, and then foisted off on Alaina at one of her oddball parties. He was approximately the size of a sequoia and very nearly as intelligent as one.

Predictably, Jayne defended him. "He's not a bad guy once you get to know him."

"Jayne, you would say that about anybody. You would say that about Adolf Hitler. You would say that about the Marquis de Sade."

Jayne made a face. "What did Knute do?"

"He took me to a wet T-shirt contest in a biker

bar. I had to threaten him with a broken beer bottle to keep him from signing me up as a contestant. You can't imagine how disappointed he was. In spite of the fact that I didn't get doused, he announced to one and all that I had far and away the best hooters in the place."

Jayne choked on her muffin. Her eyes watered. "I admit, he's a little rough around the edges."

"A little?" Alaina arched a dark brow sardonically. " 'Ill bet you like to be on top' is a long way from being a smooth line in my book."

Jayne pressed a fist to her mouth and glanced away, her cheeks turning red with pent-up laughter. "I suppose Dylan seemed like a great match after that, huh?"

Something in her tone of voice caught Alaina's attention. She prided herself on being able to read people. It was essential to success in her business. A look, a muscle twitch, a slip of the tongue—each could be a giveaway of something important in a client or a witness. And Jayne's voice carried something other than amusement. It was something subtle, something odd. Alaina gave her friend a shrewd look.

Swallowing her laughter, Jayne glanced around, casting about frantically for a new topic. Her eyes settled on Alaina's canvas and she pointed to it as if it had just suddenly sprouted up from the floor of the porch. "I like your painting. A dog with a horn. Very symbolic."

Alaina stared at the canvas. "It's a horse."

"Are you sure?"

"Of course I'm sure."

Her artistic rendition wasn't exactly a dead ringer for Fury, she admitted objectively. In fact, it had to be the ugliest horse ever immortalized in art. It had four stubby legs that all appeared to be on the same side of its body, and it definitely had the head of a Doberman.

Jayne pushed herself up from the swing and stepped closer to scrutinize the damp canvas. She narrowed her eyes and chewed her full lower lip. "Maybe subconsciously you wanted to paint a picture of a dog with a horn. Art comes from the subconscious, you know. You really shouldn't try to make the cosmic flow of creativity conform to conscious precepts."

"It's just a painting, Jayne," Alaina muttered crossly. "Don't make a big federal case out of it."

"Hello, ladies!"

The simple salutation jolted all of Alaina's sensual systems into high gear. Her head snapped up, and her gaze collided with Dylan's as he jogged up her sidewalk. He wore a pair of red running shorts that made him look impossibly tan and impossibly sexy, not just because he had great legs, but because shorts were the only clothes he had on.

His upper torso was wonderfully bare except for the thicket of dark curls that carpeted his chest and the patch of silky-looking hair on his belly. He looked damn good for a forty-year-old guy, Alaina marveled, her gaze taking in taut, flat muscles. From his chest to the tips of his running shoes, there didn't appear to be a spare ounce on him. She unconsciously sucked in her tummy as he bounded up the steps onto her porch.

Jayne beamed a smile at him. "Hello, handsome."

"Hi, Jayne." He stopped mere inches from Alaina, leaned down, and dropped a kiss on her mouth. "Good morning, Princess."

"Ummm..." She really did mean to say something, but her brain was stuck in neutral. The warmth of his mouth clung to her lips, and his taste lingered as well—mint toothpaste. "Ummm..."

"Honestly, Alaina," Jayne chuckled. "You sound like one of my llamas."

Dylan grinned, more than a little pleased with Alaina's reaction to his surprise attack. "Speechless, Counselor? I guess I've still got the magic touch."

"You do okay...for an old guy. What brings you to this neighborhood?"

"Exercise, Princess," he said, jogging in place for a few steps. "You ought to give it a try before desk-jockey spread sets in."

He had the audacity to emphasize his statement by smacking her on the fanny, then letting his fingers linger just a bare second longer than was strictly necessary. Alaina would have come back at him with a scathing remark, but she was too busy trying to gulp down a breath. The feel of his hand on her bottom had done something diabolical to her lungs.

"I'll have to take you running with me one of

these mornings," Dylan said. He planted both hands at his waist. "Fresh air, exercise, get those old endorphins flowing, flush some of the tar and nicotine out of your system. You'll love it."

Alaina shot him a look. "Get real."

"The most physical thing Alaina does is run the fax machine at work," Jayne said.

"I object to exercise on principle," she explained with her most regal look, tilting her nose up. "It makes me sweat."

Dylan waggled his brows. His voice dropped to the velvety, sexy purr that set all of Alaina's most strategic nerve endings humming. "Some of the best activities in life make us sweat, Princess."

"Speak for yourself, Conan."

How she had managed to say anything at all was beyond her. Her brain was suddenly writhing with sweaty images, every one of them erotic and every one of them involving Dylan Harrison. It wasn't difficult to imagine that he would be fantastic in bed. Most of his muscled body was visible to the eye right now, and the red running shorts didn't leave a whole lot to the imagination.

Dylan backed her up against the porch railing

and bent to nip at her pearl-studded earlobe. "Oh, I just love all those barbaric little pet names you have for me, honey muffin."

"Laying it on a bit thick, aren't you?" Alaina asked under her breath, ignoring the urge to wrap her arms around him and start doing some nibbling of her own. This was an act for Jayne's benefit, she reminded herself.

Dylan gave her his devil's smile and stepped back. "The picnic tomorrow is potluck. I volunteered us to bring potato salad. Thought I'd better tell you so you could get busy in the kitchen."

Alaina arched a brow. "You expect me to *cook*?"

"Well"—Dylan frowned—"it's just potato salad."

The silence that accompanied her look was telling. Dylan felt his heart sink a little. She couldn't cook. He wondered if she'd ever even heard of Donna Reed. He had really been hoping she would surprise him and tell him she was into gourmet cuisine. Even nouvelle would have been preferable to no talent at all.

Jayne patted his arm consolingly. "Honey, if it

doesn't have microwave instructions on the box, you're out of luck."

"I can do it," Alaina said defensively.

It was a bald-faced lie, but she didn't care. She didn't like the feeling of feminine inadequacy she'd felt facing Dylan's obvious disappointment in her lack of culinary skills. It was just potato salad. How hard could it be? She had two degrees from the University of Notre Dame, for crying out loud. She could sure as hell handle a little potato salad.

Dylan was dubious. The look of absolute shock on Jayne's face was enough to make anyone skeptical. But Alaina had her lovely chin set at that angle he recognized as mule-quality stubbornness, and there was a strange light in her eyes. She looked very determined and very vulnerable, as if she really needed to have him believe in her ability to make a stupid potato salad. His heart ached a little at that look. He had to fight to keep from wrapping his arms around her.

He was falling for her like a ton of bricks. The realization had roused him from a fitful sleep before dawn. He had sat bolt upright amid tangled sheets, his body shining with a film of cold sweat. He wasn't just physically attracted to Alaina Montgomery. There was that rare extra something to this feeling. Either he was coming down with a stomach virus, or he was falling for Alaina "I'm a career woman" Montgomery. A woman who couldn't even make potato salad.

"I'll do it," she said. The words sounded ominously like a threat.

"If it's no trouble," Dylan said tenderly, lifting a hand to rub at a smudge of black paint on her cheek.

"It's no trouble at all," Alaina murmured, her gaze still locked on his as the pad of his thumb moved in lazy circles near the corner of her mouth.

This is weird, she thought. That wavelength of awareness was buzzing between them again even though this was hardly a romantic moment. She doubted the discussion of potato salad moved even the most domestic of women to passion.

"Alaina turned loose in a kitchen?" Jayne mumbled, winding her hands in the tails of her shirt. "Sounds like big-time trouble to me."

"Don't you have to go ride your llamas or something?" Alaina asked with a pointed look.

"You don't ride llamas."

"Then whatever it is one does with llamas—shouldn't you be doing it, Jayne Emilia?"

Jayne winced and bent over the porch swing to gather up her nail polish and the enormous canvas bag she called a purse. "Okay, I can take a hint. You don't have to resort to middle-name calling." She waved to them as she backed toward the steps. "Y'all have fun at the picnic tomorrow. Alaina, call me if you change your mind about Knute."

Alaina rolled her eyes.

Dylan turned toward her with a strangely fierce expression. "Who's Knute?"

Alaina bent to pick up her palette and brush again, a slow smile tugging at her lips. That was certainly an interesting timbre in his voice. "Knute Grabowski? Just a friend," she said nonchalantly. "He's...big in the lumber business. It's nothing, really."

Dylan frowned, scratching his chest absently. A lumber baron. He didn't like the sound of that.

Without giving his actions much forethought, he reached out, turned Alaina around, and pulled her into his arms. Whether she opened her mouth out of surprise or to protest he never found out, because he took full advantage of the situation to kiss the cotton anklets off her.

His lips settled firmly against her lips, and his tongue swept against hers with lazy familiarity. Holy Hannah, she tasted good! Warm and sweet and more than a little willing. She twisted in his arms, not to escape but to get closer. Her arms crept up around his neck, the action lifting her full breasts up and rubbing them against his bare chest.

Dylan groaned his pleasure. He let one hand slide down the supple curve of her back to her hip, caressing her through her khaki walking shorts. He pulled her closer, nestling her against the cradle of his maleness.

Her brain devoid of reason or that famous control of hers, Alaina melted against him. It seemed all he had to do was touch her, and she was transformed from a rational, practical person to a featherheaded ninny.

When he finally lifted his head, she looked up at him, dazed. Dylan Harrison had just kissed her senseless on her front porch in front of God and everybody. Two teenagers biking past had stopped by her curb to watch.

"What was that for?" she asked weakly.

Careful what you say, Harrison, you're going to blow it, he warned himself. Alaina claimed she wasn't interested in anything other than a phony relationship. If he even hinted at what kissing her meant to him, she was going to hand him his walking papers.

He grinned wickedly and tapped a finger against the tip of her patrician nose. "Practice. We want to be convincing, don't we?"

Yes, but who was he trying to convince now? she wondered.

"Nice painting," he said as he sauntered toward the steps. "A dog with a horn. I like it."

He just managed to dodge the paintbrush that sailed at his head.

"See you tomorrow, Princess," he said with a chuckle.

Chapter 5

Alaina wasn't sure what she had imagined a bar and bait shop would look like, but the reality was a pleasant surprise. Dylan's was a tidy-looking place with weathered gray siding decorated with all manner of seagoing paraphernalia. Fishnets were draped artistically between life rings and anchors. The signboard swinging above the main door on an iron bracket read simply DYLAN'S BAR AND BAIT SHOP in jaunty blue letters. There was a wooden tub beside the entrance overflowing with fuchsia petunias. The building had been constructed right on a pier in Anastasia's thriving marina district, an area that was buzzing with activity on this perfect fall morning.

Slinging her purse over her shoulder, Alaina scooped her container of potato salad off the front seat of her car and headed for the bar—peeling the deli price tag off as she went. It wasn't as if she hadn't tried to make the damn stuff herself, she reflected as she rolled the gummed tag into a little ball and tucked it beneath a petunia in the tub beside the door. The current state of her kitchen was a testament to the fact that she had indeed made a valiant if unsuccessful effort. The taste of defeat was still bitter in her mouth.

She took a deep breath before stepping inside, trying to still the jittering nerves in her belly. What did she have to be nervous about? She was going to meet Dylan's employees and his children. They were going on a nice, simple picnic. As far as social occasions went, she'd handled a lot tougher gigs than this one.

The interior of the bar was much like the exterior—weathered gray boards and a fishing motif. She had half-expected mismatched chairs and battered tables crowded with hulking, smelly fishermen. What she found were neatly kept, relatively new furnishings, a floor clean enough to eat off, and a handsome bar area with shelves of bottles behind it. A door at the far end of the room had the words BAIT SHOP stenciled on the glass, obviously leading to the second, less appetizing half of the business.

Dylan sat behind the bar, a blue T-shirt with the place's logo on it spanning his chest and broad shoulders. He was bent over the keyboard of a personal computer, tapping keys as he spoke with a stocky man dressed in jeans and a Windbreaker.

"I think a tax-deferred annuity is the answer, Miguel," he said. "Precious metals can be lucrative, but they can be risky too. I've got a bad feeling about the gold market right now."

"If you think this is best, my friend," Miguel said in broken English, nodding his dark head.

"I'll take care of it first thing Monday."

"Tax-deferred annuities?" Alaina questioned when Miguel had gone. "I thought all a person could get in a place like this was rotgut whiskey and chopped-up fish."

"Caught in the act," Dylan said with a rather

sheepish grin on his wide mouth. "Um ... I used to work for Drexel-Barnhart," he said almost apologetically as he pulled his wire-rimmed reading glasses off and rubbed the bridge of his nose.

Alaina's brows rose at the name of the prestigious investment firm. Dylan Harrison of the hula girl tie and high-top sneakers working for a button-down-collar, gray-flannel-suit place like Drexel-Barnhart? It was difficult—no, impossible—to believe.

"I had shorter hair then," he said, as if that would clear everything up.

A wry smile lifted the corner of Alaina's mouth. "Unpretentious, unambitious, unmaterialistic Dylan Harrison at Drexel-Barnhart?"

"That was before I saw the light," he said in a superior tone.

If he was so enlightened, then what was he doing discussing annuities with Miguel? she wondered. It looked to her as if Dylan wasn't completely reformed of his yuppie ways. The look she slanted him told him as much.

"I do a little on the side now, just for friends,"

he explained defensively as he shut down his computer, uncomfortable with the topic and with Alaina's sharp-eyed scrutiny. Rising from his chair, he spied the container in her hands. "That the potato salad?"

She nodded, still trying to recover from the shock of discovering Dylan was a closet investment counselor.

"Did you have any trouble with it?"

"No, not a bit." That girl behind the deli counter had just scooped it right out, no problem, she thought. There had been a tense moment deciding between the kind with hard-boiled eggs and the kind with shredded carrots, but other than that the mission had gone smoothly.

"Let's get it in the cooler," Dylan said, motioning for her to follow him, "then we can load up the boat. Everyone should be here soon."

"Boat?" Alaina questioned weakly as Dylan rounded the corner of the bar and took the plastic container from her suddenly numb fingers. "What boat?"

He peeked inside the dish and made a face of surprised approval. "My boat. The *Tardis*."

"You never said anything about a boat."

"Didn't I?" He shrugged. "Oh, well."

Oh, well?

Dylan gave her a curious look. "You've been on a boat before, haven't you, Princess?"

"Sure," she managed, scraping up a bare ounce of bravado. "Of course I've been on a boat."

She'd been on a boat. Once. On Lake Michigan with stepfather number two, Harold the ball-bearing manufacturer. She couldn't remember which aspect had been the worst—Harold, the seasickness, or the sun poisoning.

"The picnic is on the boat," Dylan explained.

He led her out a side door to a wide area of the pier that was shaded this time of day. Round white tables with collapsed blue umbrellas nestled against the side of the building, waiting for customers and a romantic sunset.

Dylan knelt down beside an enormous brown cooler and tucked the potato salad inside. "We'll go up the coast a ways to this little cove, drop anchor, eat, and fish. It's a nice, relaxing way to spend the day."

"Who minds the bar?" Alaina asked, strongly

considering volunteering for the task. "What if someone comes in and wants to order up a beer or some T-bills or something?"

"We're closed for the day. It's kind of hard to have an employee picnic if half the employees are working. That's the beauty of being unmaterialistic," he said smugly, spreading his arms in an expansive shrug. "It doesn't matter to me if I miss a day's profits."

Alaina rolled her eyes. The boat tied up alongside the dock caught her attention. The *Tardis*. She was no expert, but it looked pretty sharp to her. It looked as if Dylan could afford to miss a day's profits. She would have commented on this if she hadn't been so dismayed at the prospect of spending the day on the deck of the gleaming craft.

Dylan studied Alaina's pallor with interest. She was looking at the *Tardis* as if it were a sea monster that might just swallow her whole. It seemed the invincible woman had a chink in her armor. Rather than finding it disappointing, he found it oddly endearing. Gently he asked,

"Alaina, you're not worried about going out in the boat, are you?"

"Of course not," she said, tipping her chin up and fighting the urge to gag as the smell of fish wafted down from the area where the commercial boats were moored. "It's just that—that—the life jacket will clash with my outfit. You should have warned me."

"I don't think you'll offend too many people," Dylan said dryly. He eyed what she was wearing— a silky pink tank top and a trendy pair of tan jodhpurs. A slow, sexy smile spread across his mouth. "Alai-na, you're wearing fuch-sia," he singsonged, reaching out to run his forefinger just under the strap of the blouse. His voice dropped a velvety octave as his gaze locked on hers. "It's very pretty. Did you wear this just for me?"

Alaina's normally nimble tongue stumbled on her answer, giving her away almost as surely as her blush did. She managed a lame "No," but Dylan obviously didn't buy it. That she came up with an answer at all was a minor miracle considering the alarming rush of feelings the languid caress of his fingertip had brought on. He dragged it lazily up and down along the strap of her blouse, coming alarmingly close to the upper swell of her left breast.

It irked her that she hadn't been able to smoothly deny his assumption—almost as badly as it irked that she had indeed chosen the silky tank top with Dylan's unusual color preference in mind. It wasn't like her to dress to please a man. She couldn't for the life of her figure out why she had done so today.

Dylan realized he was grinning like an idiot. He didn't care. Alaina had dressed to please him. Never mind that her outfit would have been more appropriate for a Ralph Lauren fashion shoot. Never mind that she was there ostensibly as part of their deal. The more he saw of Alaina, the less he thought about the mundane practicality of their arrangement. That may not have been wise, but it was the truth.

He wondered now what she would do if he repeated his performance of yesterday and kissed her. Heaven knew he'd thought of little else since the encounter on her porch. There hadn't been anything mundane in her response. A pleasant kind of heat flushed his skin at the thought.

The side screen door slammed and Cori and Sam wandered out onto the pier, escorted by their big shaggy dog and a middle-aged woman with a dyed-red beehive hairdo.

Dylan jerked his hand away from Alaina's shoulder as if her skin had burned him. Clearing his throat and pasting on a nervous smile, he hurried to introduce her to his family.

"Alaina, this is our housekeeper, Mrs. Phoebe Pepoon. My son, Sam, and my daughter, Cori." The dog whined and barked at him. "Oh—ah—and our dog, Scottie. Everybody, this is my friend, Alaina Montgomery."

Alaina smiled politely and nodded from one to the next of the troop.

Phoebe Pepoon had a rather disconcertingly vacuous expression, a crooked, tight-lipped smile, and eyeglasses with lens so thick they made her green eyes look huge and watery. An enormous woven straw tote slung over her shoulder was overflowing with tubes of sunscreen.

"It's a pleasure to meet you, Ms. Montgomery,"

Sam said soberly, stepping forward to shake Alaina's hand. "Dad was right, you do bear a pronounced parallelism of visual perspective to Princess Andora."

Alaina blinked. "Umm—thank you . . . I think."

"Pas de quoi," he said with a flawless accent.

Dylan shrugged almost apologetically. "He just bought a 'Teach Yourself French' cassette."

Alaina nodded, managing a stunned smile. "I see."

Nine going on forty-two was how Dylan had described his son. That seemed painfully accurate to Alaina. Sam had a thatch of sandy hair and a smattering of freckles. He was dressed in colorful baggy shorts and a neon-bright T-shirt, like any California kid his age. But the speculative look he gave her was nothing short of adult. She had a feeling nothing much got by Sam.

Turning slightly, Alaina looked down at Dylan's daughter, and a wall gave way deep inside her. The eyes she gazed into may have been darker than her own, but they were an absolute reflection of her own at seven years of age—wary, hurt, vulnerable. Alaina saw in Cori Harrison not only an adorable little moppet with curly dark hair, but a soul mate, a child who had had the foundation of her life cracked by divorce.

She gave the girl a small, empathetic smile. Cori didn't smile back, but turned and looked up at her brother, who held her hand. She was looking to Sam for a sign, and it was clear that Sam was reserving judgment.

Alaina felt a pang of rejection, but it was tempered by understanding. She could well remember the parade of men her mother had introduced to her over the years of her childhood. She had learned very quickly that a friendly smile for her was often meant to garner brownie points with Helene. She hadn't trusted any easier than Cori or Sam did.

Dylan watched the exchange with interest, his attention focusing mainly on Alaina. He had been very nervous wondering what her reaction to his kids would be. Alaina did not strike him as being overly maternal. That had worried him for a variety of reasons. But what he saw in her expression now was something other than polite interest. In fact, she appeared to be lost in thought as she looked down at Cori and Sam.

Heaven help him, she looked vulnerable again, he thought with a sinking feeling in the pit of his stomach. That look always came as such a surprise to him. Alaina's image was one of the tough, confident professional. To see her vulnerable, to know that under that slick, polished exterior she was capable of being vulnerable, had a profound impact on his heart.

There was so much more to Alaina than what so pleasingly met the eye. She had given him a glimpse of the woman behind the shield of cool self-sufficiency when she'd made the telling remark about her mother the other night. Now she was giving him a glimpse of the lonely girl she must have been. Dylan wanted to know more. He wanted to know everything about her. He wanted to uncover all her secrets. He had decided the ruse of their phony relationship was going to give him the opportunity to do just that.

* * *

The *Tardis* was a good-sized boat—or was it a ship? *Who cares?* Alaina thought as her stomach rose and fell with the sea. It wasn't big enough. The *Queen Elizabeth II* might have been big enough. At least the *Queen Elizabeth* had cabins where a miserably seasick person could hide until death blissfully descended upon her.

She looked around the deck, careful not to move her head, just her eyeballs. No one else appeared to be suffering any ill effects. Cori and Sam, swallowed up in their puffy orange life jackets, trotted around on the deck as if it were motionless. Scottie the dog, also sporting a life preserver, trailed happily after them with a big doggie grin on his face.

Mrs. Pepoon, wearing clip-on sunglasses, her nose and lips coated white with zinc oxide, sat at the very front of the boat, staring out at the sea, an abstract, updated version of the carvings that adorned the bows of wooden ships of old. *She must be one hell of a housekeeper,* Alaina thought, because she certainly couldn't see any other reason for employing such an odd woman.

Rita, the bar's head waitress, and her no-neck,

commercial-fisherman husband, Cleve, were dancing to the music that poured out of a boom box, and—Alaina gulped hard—drinking beer. Under the best of circumstances her stomach rejected beer. The mere thought of it now had her shuddering.

Chloe, Cleve's identical twin sister, sat in a deck chair next to the cooler, enthusiastically bent over a plate of food. Alaina winced a little at the thought of Dylan's having to fend off a bruiser like Chloe. Poor guy. Bulging with muscles, Chloe looked like the poster girl for steroid abuse. She glanced up from her lunch and smiled at Alaina, swiping a spot of mayonnaise out of her mustache. "Good potato salad, Alaina."

Forcing an anemic smile, Alaina said, "Thanks." *I bought it myself.*

"Is it a family recipe?"

"Yes." Of the Liebowitz family, proprietors of the Fourth Street Deli.

"How's it going, Counselor?" Dylan emerged from belowdecks with several fishing poles. He set them down carefully and leaned back against the railing where Alaina stood looking ready to turn and heave her breakfast overboard. He slid an arm around her waist and snuggled her against his side, giving her a wink and a short nod in Chloe's direction.

"Super," Alaina said without much enthusiasm. "Wonderful."

Chloe didn't look all that interested to her. The waitress seemed more enamored of the contents of the ice chest than she was enamored of Dylan. She was reaching for her third sandwich.

"She's an interesting lady," Alaina murmured.

"Chloe? Yeah." Dylan kept his voice low and conspiratorial, one eye trained on his waitress as if he were afraid she might suddenly bolt and charge. "She was a Marine, you know. Took two years before anyone found out she was a woman. It made all the papers."

Alaina gave him a look. "Harrison, you are so full of it."

A sharp swell lifted the boat. By the look on her face Dylan figured Alaina's stomach had lodged itself somewhere in the vicinity of her tonsils. He watched her grit her teeth, and he had to smile to himself. She was a trooper, poor sweetheart. She wasn't the least bit comfortable on the sea, but killer whales wouldn't have been able to drag that admission out of her.

"You're sure you're all right?" he asked gently, lifting a hand to tenderly comb her dark hair back from her pale cheek. "You're looking a little green."

Alaina willed her mutinous breakfast to settle. For some reason it seemed extremely important that she pass this test. She didn't want Dylan thinking she couldn't handle the seagoing life. The reason she didn't want him thinking it made her stomach roll all the more, because she had a sinking feeling it wasn't just a matter of her being highly competitive. It was a matter of wanting to please him.

She took a slow, deep breath. "It's...my makeup. The woman at Elizabeth Arden specifically told me it would take on a greenish cast if I went out on the ocean."

"Oh, well, maybe it would tone down a bit if you ate a little something." The horrified look she gave Dylan tugged at his heartstrings. He bent down and pressed a kiss to the tip of her nose. "Have a piece of bread," he murmured, briefly savoring the feel of her sagging against him. "Trust me."

Trust him? Alaina nearly laughed out loud. She had trusted him to take her on an innocuous little picnic, and there she was, ready to toss her cookies into the heaving Pacific. The man was a menace, she thought, looking up at him. He was also right at home on a boat—ship—whatever.

The sea breeze ruffled his wavy chestnut hair and kissed his high cheekbones with healthy color. His hair was far too long to be fashionable among her crowd, Alaina thought, but she wouldn't have had him change it. The unruly locks were part of who he was—just as this floating nausea machine was. She groaned inwardly as he led her to a chair.

The bread actually helped, enough that Alaina managed to try several of the dishes Dylan's friends had brought along. She ate her lunch without paying much attention to it, all the while keeping an appreciative eye on Dylan. He had stripped off his T-shirt and tied his hair at the nape of his neck with a shoelace, making him look like an eighteenth-century pirate captain. Sun-bronzed muscles rippled as he worked around the boat seeing to the needs of his compatriots.

In addition to Rita, Cleve, and Chloe, there were two old-timers who worked in the bait shop and a Russian defector named Uri who helped tend bar. They were an unusual group, to be sure. Unfortunately, being able to eat and keep food down seemed to be the only thing Alaina had in common with Dylan's crew.

It was plain she didn't fit in with his friends. They were from blue-collar backgrounds, and try as she might, Alaina could find no comfortable way into their conversations. Her comments were met with polite but cool responses or blank looks. She got the distinct impression they would rather Dylan had left her behind.

His children didn't seem to think much of her either. Cori and Sam avoided her like the plague, though several times she caught them watching her from a distance. Scottie the dog ran off with her Gucci handbag and chewed a hole in it before Dylan could wrest it away from him.

All in all, Alaina thought as she sat beside the

reticent Mrs. Pepoon later that afternoon, her first effort at "keeping company" with Dylan was an unqualified failure. After tangling herself in fishing line and snagging her silk blouse with a hook, she had been banned from the angling activities. She wasn't keeping company with Dylan at all, she thought morosely, her gaze straying to Phoebe Pepoon. She was keeping company with a woman with a beehive hairdo and orange polyester pedal pushers.

Depression settled over her like a pall as she watched Dylan helping his children fish. She'd never felt so rotten in all her adult life. What was the matter with her? She had never before considered it a problem that she didn't fit in with commercial fishermen and bait-shop waitresses. It had never mattered that children didn't flock around her for attention. Coordination with a fishing pole had never been high on her list of priorities.

The reason hit her smack between the eyes when Dylan glanced back at her, winked, and waved. Cold reality intensified her depression to gigantic proportions.

She wanted to be accepted by Dylan's friends,

she wanted to be accepted by Dylan's children, because she wanted to be accepted by Dylan.

She was falling for him.

Panic crashed over her like a tsunami wave. It was her most secret wish sneaking up on her and viciously attacking her without warning. Way down deep inside her, beneath the resilient toughness, beyond the cool self-possession, she had always harbored the desire to be a part of a normal, loving family—like Dylan's family.

"Oh, no," she whispered, appalled by the prickle of tears at the back of her eyes.

This had to be the worst possible thing that could have happened! She couldn't fall for Dylan Harrison! They had made a deal; this was to be a relationship in name only. He had told her she was perfect for the job because she wasn't his type of woman at all. There was no chance of his really falling for her on a long-term basis. Dylan wanted a woman who could fish. He wanted a woman who could make potato salad. He had no desire to hook up with another career woman.

In a daze, Alaina stared across the deck at him. Her heart gave a great, traitorous *ker-thump* as she watched him kneel down beside Cori's chair and wrap his arms around his little girl—the little girl with the big, sad eyes. A lump the size of an Idaho russet lodged in Alaina's throat.

Oh, Lord, she thought, pressing a carefully manicured hand to her trembling lips, she was falling in love with him.

No question. This was definitely breach of contract.

Of all the bloody rotten luck! Alaina ground her teeth, anger intermingling with all the other raw emotions inside her. She didn't want to be in love with Dylan Harrison. She didn't want to be in love with anybody, she vowed, locking that secret dream back in its box in the farthest corner of her heart. For years she had prided herself on being practical, levelheaded, and patently unromantic. That was the image she had always wanted to project. Love was a tenuous, fickle, silly thing. She didn't want anything to do with it.

"You're looking a little out of sorts, Princess," Dylan said, taking Mrs. Pepoon's chair as his housekeeper made her way belowdecks. He dropped his blue baseball cap on Alaina's head and pushed the bill down low over her eyes. "Did you and Mrs. Pepoon have a fight?"

Pushing the cap up, Alaina leaned away from him, only vertigo keeping her from getting up and moving to another chair. Being within touching distance of Dylan didn't seem like a good idea at the moment. Falling overboard seemed marginally worse. "It's rather difficult to fight with someone who hasn't uttered a word to me all day."

"Difficult, but it can be done," he said, thinking back to the cold war Veronica had waged during their marriage when she had wanted to move to L.A. and he had wanted to move to Anastasia. He eyed Alaina carefully. She had her pretty patrician nose out of joint about something.

"This isn't precisely my element, you know." Inner tension clipped her words.

"You're not having a good time?" It was more a flat statement than a question.

She gave him one of her stony looks in answer.

Dylan felt a renewal of the anxiety he had experienced earlier. A blind person could have seen Alaina was having a lousy time. After a few half-hearted attempts to fit in with his friends and his children, she had withdrawn. That was not a good sign.

He couldn't find it in him to blame her, though. He'd dragged her on a boat and gotten her seasick. One of his fishhooks had ruined the blouse she'd worn for him—silk by Anne Klein, ninety-seven fifty. His dog had eaten her purse—leather by Gucci, one hundred sixty-five dollars. Those incidents didn't add up to a fun day in anyone's book. They probably added up to a huge black mark against him in Alaina's. She already swore he wasn't her type. He'd spent the day proving it and running up a bill as well.

Dylan heaved a sigh.

Another problem he hadn't foreseen was the cold shoulder his friends had turned Alaina's way. True, Alaina hadn't made much of an effort to fit in, but his staff hadn't exactly extended open arms either. He supposed they were bent out of shape over the fact that he had chosen Alaina himself rather than letting them foist someone off on him.

Being a bachelor could be damned complicated.

"You don't have to give up your fishing just to

keep me company," Alaina said, too busy trying to disguise the suspicious thickness in her voice to realize the words she'd used.

"Part of the deal, isn't it, Princess?" he said softly, rubbing a finger gently under her down-tilted chin.

"You'd rather be with your friends."

"You're my friend."

He said it with such simplicity of feeling, it brought tears to her eyes. Alaina cursed herself for this latent sentimental streak that was surfacing in her. She couldn't imagine where it was coming from. She wasn't sentimental. She didn't cry in front of people. She didn't fall for men who played the baritone and wore their hair in queues.

"In spite of a few minor problems, I think we've been very successful today. Chloe seems to have taken the hint," Dylan said. Poor Chloe. She'd flatten him if she knew the way he'd been taking her name in vain.

Alaina arched a brow. "Yes," she said dryly. "Unless you're overcome by a sudden urge to recline between two slices of bread, I think you'll be safe."

Dylan chuckled, reaching over to flip up the bill on the cap Alaina was still wearing. His expression dropped abruptly and he leaned over to take a closer look at her face. His brows lifted in alarm. His brown eyes rounded in shock.

"What?" Alaina questioned cautiously.

"You're puffing up."

"I'm what?"

"Puffing up. Your face—it's sort of—" He motioned around his own face, filling his lean, tanned cheeks with air.

Alaina's heart went into overdrive. Frantically she dug through her mangled handbag for her compact, relieved to find Scottie hadn't ingested it. She popped the sterling-silver case open and held up the little mirror.

Dylan was right. She was puffing up. Her face was swelling before her very eyes. Her normally flawless fair skin was taking on a weird, red-mottled look.

With a strangled cry of shock she fell back into her deck chair.

* * *

"I'm really sorry about that crab salad, Alaina," Rita said, a look of genuine concern in her eyes as she followed Dylan and Alaina down the gangplank from the *Tardis*. "I had no idea you were allergic."

Alaina waved a puffed-up hand at the petite blond woman. "It's not your fault, Rita. I should have been paying closer attention to what I was eating."

"Dad, do we have to go home?" Sam asked irritably. "It's not our fault *she* got sick. Couldn't you just leave her, and we could go back out?"

Dylan gave his son a look burning with parental opinions, none of which he voiced. Poor Alaina was miserable enough without having a family fight ensue over her.

"I'm taking Alaina home. You guys can stay here with Mrs. Pepoon and play video games in the bar if you like."

"You don't have to take me home," Alaina protested, waddling up the dock. Her feet had swelled so quickly, she couldn't even begin to get them out of her alligator wingtips.

Dylan was adamant. "You can't drive in this

condition. Besides, I want to make sure you get home and get that medication into you. Who knows what could happen with this allergy? You could become delirious or pass out or something."

Alaina shook her head. "All I do is puff up. I'd rather not have an audience, thank you very much."

Tears welled up in her eyes—eyes that had become tiny blue beads staring out between pooched-out cheeks and puffed-up eyelids. All she wanted to do was go home and hide for the rest of her natural life.

She fumbled in her ruined purse for her keys, but wasn't able to close her swollen fingers around them. Swearing a blue streak, she hurled the Gucci bag at her BMW and set off the alarm, drawing the eyes of at least a hundred people who were wandering around the marina area.

"Lovely." She growled the word between her teeth. "Just lovely."

Chapter 6

"Marlene warned me about this," Alaina grumbled, fuming.

Dylan piloted the BMW onto Alaina's street and turned in at her driveway. Consciously, he was wincing. Alaina was in a rare fine temper, and he couldn't seem to stop blaming himself for some idiotic reason, as if he'd force-fed her Rita's crab salad. Subconsciously, he was enjoying the feel of fine German engineering beneath him and telling himself that didn't make him a materialist.

"Marlene told me not to go today. She said my moon was in the wrong house. I told her to mind her own moon."

"I thought you didn't believe in malarkey."

"I don't. But now I'm going to have to listen to Marlene say 'I told you so' for the next thousand years." She huffed a sigh of pure annoyance. "The woman is insufferable."

"Then why do you put up with her?"

"Because I like her, dammit."

Turning off the ignition, Dylan sat back against the plush leather seat and bit back a chuckle. He rubbed a hand across the smile that threatened. This was no time to find the lady amusing.

Slowly he turned toward her, his eyes tearing up at the effort to keep from laughing. "You're home now, Princess. You can take the bag off your head."

Alaina lifted the edge of the brown paper sack and peeked out at him. "Are you sure the coast is clear?"

"Alaina, you don't look that bad—"

"I look like the Elephant Woman," she said flatly. "And I want to make this crystal clear—if *one* neighbor sees me, Dylan Harrison, I will cut out your heart with a penknife."

He made a great show of looking all around with his hand raised to his forehead to make a visor. "There isn't a neighbor in sight."

Alaina slipped the grocery bag off her head and folded it with quick efficiency. She felt like a fool. Dylan probably thought she was the vainest creature on Earth. Well, fine. He could just add vanity to her list of faults, which now included being unseaworthy and inept with a fishing pole.

Depression weighed on her like a millstone as she got out of the car, and she muttered a string of expletives under her breath. Since when had she aspired to become an angler? Lord, the very idea of touching a live fish sent her into the shudders. Until Dylan, the nearest she'd ever cared to get to a fish was the fork side of a plate of grilled fillet of sole.

They nearly made it into the house. Alaina had just begun to breathe a sigh of relief when Marlene's front door swung open. Her secretary bolted onto the porch, wild-eyed as she took in Alaina's bloated appearance. She stared in silence for a long ten seconds, her hands clutching at the voluminous folds of her enormous 49ers jersey.

Abruptly she shook off her stunned trance and shook a stubby finger at Alaina, bracelets rattling on her wrist. "I told you your moon was in the wrong house."

Alaina narrowed her eyes until they were nearly invisible. "Nip it, Marlene. Just nip it."

Undaunted, Marlene planted her fists on her hips. "I'll bring over some herbal potions."

"That's okay, Marlene," Dylan said, unlocking Alaina's front door. "We can handle everything. Thanks anyway."

"You're sure?"

"Yeah. She'll be fine in no time." He paused as he remembered Alaina's threat about the penknife. "But if you happen to hear me screaming, dial nine one one."

Alaina glared at him as Dylan ushered her through the door into the air-conditioned comfort of her lovely, quiet home.

"Marlene doesn't count as a neighbor, does she?"

"Don't worry," Alaina grumbled. "I wouldn't know a penknife if I stepped on one."

"So your bark is worse than your bite, eh,

Princess?" Dylan grinned at the venomous look on her face. "Where do you keep your allergy medication?"

"In the kitchen cupboard, left of the sink."

No sooner had the words left her swollen lips than she wished them back. Her kitchen, she remembered too late, looked like the aftermath of a major disaster because of her aborted attempt at making potato salad. Feeling utterly dejected, she slumped down into a rose-pink chair that was nearly as overstuffed as she was.

Dylan returned a few minutes later with a prescription bottle, a glass of water, and a pair of kitchen shears. He said not one word about the holocaust he'd found in the kitchen or the big note tacked up by the egg-splattered kitchen phone that read: LIEBOWITZ'S FOURTH STREET DELI HAS POTATO SALAD. THANK GOD! He handed Alaina the pills and water, then knelt at her feet.

"What are you doing?" she asked, eyeing the scissors he held.

"I'm cutting these shoes off."

Several fat tears spilled over the barrier of her thick lashes. "Those are my favorite shoes," she murmured sadly. "Real alligator. Three hundred twenty-five dollars. My name is stamped inside them in gold leaf."

Dylan scowled. "Would you rather lose your shoes or your feet?"

Alaina bit her lip, considering.

"Put it on my tab," he said. Grumbling something disparaging about the yuppie mentality, Dylan took matters into his own hands. The shoes were dispensed with and disposed of in the kitchen garbage can along with what looked like five gallons of mayonnaise and twenty pounds of overcooked potatoes.

He shook his head as he stared at the mess, caught between laughing and groaning. Alaina really had tried to make the stuff. She simply wasn't domestic.

With a heavy sigh he went back into the living room and pulled Alaina up out of her chair.

"Where's your bedroom?"

"Upstairs." She gave him a haughty look that was lost in her balloonlike features. "Why?"

"Because you're going to bed," Dylan announced, leading her toward the stairs. "It said on the bottle those pills will make you drowsy. And I'm staying until you fall asleep—just to make sure you don't go out and try to operate any heavy machinery."

"That's really not necessary," she protested. "There aren't any bulldozers in the neighborhood. I wouldn't be caught dead on one anyway."

"All part of the bargain, sweetheart," Dylan murmured.

The truth of the matter was, he couldn't leave her. Seeing the indomitable Alaina Montgomery puffed up and miserable, teary-eyed over a stupid pair of alligator shoes, had him all choked up. All his protective instincts were surfacing full force.

He sent her into her bathroom with her robe and wandered around her bedroom while he waited for her to come back out.

This room, like the living room, was immaculate. Like the living room, it was tastefully decorated. The floor was covered with plush rose carpet, the walls papered in a soft blue-and-rose floral pattern with the woodwork painted light blue. Rich, frothy lace draped the bay window where a rose-colored velvet cushion invited a person to curl up on the window seat to read or daydream. It touched his heart to think of Alaina daydreaming there.

Her bed was very feminine. The headboard and footboard were made of ornately curved, polished black iron with bright brass accents. The mattress was covered with a pristine-white, hand-crocheted spread. A mountain of frilly pillows leaned up against the headboard. It certainly wasn't difficult for him to picture Alaina there, her expression soft and unguarded as she slept.

This room told Dylan a lot about the woman he had grown so fond of so quickly. This room told him secrets. Art deco was the style she presented visitors in the rest of her home—spartan and stylish. In her sanctuary she preferred the feminine lines of Queen Anne in her cherry dresser and blue damask wing chair. Bold, dramatic day lilies were displayed in her living room; a small crystal vase in this room held delicate pink snapdragons and fragile violets.

This wasn't the room of a tough, cynical attorney. This was the room of a woman who was sensitive, vulnerable, perhaps a little shy. A week ago he wouldn't have said any of those words applied to Alaina. Now he didn't question the probability. He'd guessed from the first there was more to Alaina than met the eye. He was seeing it here.

There was a petite black cat curled up on the window seat, a mystery novel on the table by the bed. The bookmark indicated Alaina was halfway through the paperback, but the book's cover was smooth, unmarred, uncurled. Beside the book on the lace runner lay the Crystal of Kalamari, the wedge of glass filled with rainbows by the amber light falling through the window. Behind the Crystal stood a photograph in a sterling frame.

Dylan ran his fingertips over the coveted pin, but he didn't pick it up. Instead, he lifted the picture frame carefully and studied the photo in the fading light. He recognized Alaina and Jayne and their friend Faith Kincaid. There was a fourth person, a young man he didn't know. The four stood in graduation caps and gowns, smiling, their expressions wistful. Behind them a rainbow hung in the sky.

This was the only photograph in the room, the only one he'd seen anywhere in the house. Alaina and her college friends. He hadn't seen anything anywhere indicating that she had a family someplace. There were no snapshots of brothers or sisters because she had none. There was no portrait of her parents, no picture of the mother who'd had no time for her. It made him sad. He'd grown up in a large, happy family. The walls of his house practically bowed under the weight of all the photographs of the Harrison clan.

"I look like a blowfish," Alaina lamented as she emerged from the bathroom wrapped in her gray silk dressing gown, her bloated bare toes peeking out from under the hem.

Dylan set the photograph down and turned to face her, his heart flipping over. His fiercely proud Princess of the Zanatares looked as close to tears as anyone could come, but she blinked at them furiously in the attempt to keep them from falling.

"Oh . . ." He crossed the room to take her puffy hands in his. "It's not that bad, honey, really it's not. I think the pills are starting to help already. I can almost see your eyes."

That did it. Abruptly Alaina lost her battle. Tears gushed down her cheeks. She felt utterly miserable, rejected, humiliated, lost, and furious about it all. She stamped her foot and muttered a stream of virulent curses.

"I hate this! I just hate it! I hate being puffy and I hate being allergic and I hate crying and I hate having you see me do it!"

Dylan pulled her into his arms and held her against him, rubbing her back while she sobbed and swore. "I know, sweetheart. I know you hate it." If he hadn't already figured it out for himself, Alaina was telling him now—she didn't like anyone seeing a weakness in her. Misty-eyed, he smiled and kissed her hair. "I know, honey. You're a tough cookie."

"I am," Alaina declared, diminishing the effectiveness of her statement with a watery sniffle.

"Yeah, well, even tough cookies have to crumble every once in a while," Dylan told her. "You've had a hard day, haven't you, Princess?"

He didn't know the half of it, Alaina thought glumly as she nodded against his broad shoulder. Aside from the more obvious catastrophes, she'd gone and fallen in love with him—Dylan Harrison, all-around goofball and proprietor of a bar and bait shop, a man who had sworn to settle for nothing short of a domestic goddess in a woman. He had stayed with her, but every time he did something nice for her he had to remind her it was because he was duty-bound by the deal they had made. All things considered, a day couldn't get much worse than the one she'd just had.

"Come on, sweetheart," Dylan murmured. "What you need is a good night's sleep."

Not bothering with the pillows or bedcovers, he sat on the bed, pulling Alaina down beside him. She let him move her around as if she were a mannequin, simply not possessing the strength of will to fight him. He lifted her feet up and tipped her over so she was lying on her side facing the nightstand and the window, then he settled himself behind her, spoon-style, slipping his arm around her waist.

"You don't have to do this," she said, hoping he wouldn't agree.

"Of course I have to do this." He gave her a hug. "You don't think I'd pass on the chance to say I slept with the Elephant Woman, do you?"

Alaina couldn't help but chuckle, although the

sound didn't contain much energy. "You're a smart-ass, Harrison, and perverse in the extreme."

"I've just always had a liking for inflatable women."

"I don't doubt it."

A moment of comfortable silence passed between them. Alaina lay there relaxed and savoring the feel of Dylan snuggled behind her, solid and masculine, his arm draped over her waist.

"Feeling better?" he asked, his voice warm and soft with genuine concern.

"A little."

He really was a sweet guy. Too bad she was all wrong for him, she thought. Too bad for her, because it hurt like hell to think nothing would ever come of this arrangement they'd entered into. It was her own dumb fault. She hadn't read the fine print, hadn't considered the possibility that she might just fall in love with Dylan Harrison.

It had seemed too remote a possibility. She'd never been in love, not really. She had always sort of wondered if she was even capable of falling in love. Too many years of practice had taught her to guard her heart even while she'd still wanted someone to make the effort to win it. The risk that she might find yet another imitation of love had far outweighed the chance of stumbling across the real thing.

There had been her affair with Clayton, of course, but she had never really loved him. What she had felt for him had been mutual respect—until Mrs. Collier had turned up—and compatibility. As had been pointed out to her incessantly over the course of the last few days by Jayne and Marlene, she and Dylan didn't rank high in compatibility, but what she felt for him was love nonetheless. Nothing else could have hurt this way in the face of hopelessness.

"How stupid of me!" Dylan said suddenly.

Alaina cringed at the thought that he had no doubt been mulling over their situation too. Poor guy. She couldn't blame him for having regrets about the deal. She'd been an unqualified failure at all the things he'd wanted her to do. Just as she started to apologize, Dylan raised up on one elbow and leaned over her, reaching for something on the nightstand. Alaina's heart bolted against her ribs at the feel of his lean, hard body pressing against hers. He smelled faintly of the sea, and she wanted to turn and bury her face against his chest and have him hold her as he had earlier. She cursed herself under her breath. This was no time to develop a penchant for chasing rainbows.

"The Crystal of Kalamari," he said as he settled back down on the bed. He held the pin between his thumb and forefinger so Alaina could see the colors that burst inside it.

"Take it," he said, pressing it into her open palm. "It has all kinds of powers. All you have to do is hold it in your hand and make a wish. You'll be deflated in no time."

"Is that a fact?" Alaina said without hope. She took the bit of glass, a sad smile touching her mouth at Dylan's attempt to lighten her mood.

"Absolutely. The wizard Danathamien imbued it with the ability to heal. It can also bore a hole through the head of a cyclops, but that's another story. The point is, it's full of magic."

"Magic." The word had a very unmagical flatness coming from her lips.

"Magic," Dylan said resolutely. "I think it might do you some good to believe in magic."

Alaina almost laughed at his words, words that rang too familiar in her ears. More than once during the course of their Fearsome Foursome days, Bryan Hennessy had told her the very same thing—that she ought to believe in magic. How could she believe in it? she wondered. To date she had never seen any evidence of it in her life.

If there had been magic, then she would have grown up in a normal family with parents who loved her and Clayton Collier would never have taken advantage of her and Dylan Harrison would think of her as something other than a means to an end.

If there were magic, she thought as she closed her fist around the warm vee of glass and closed her eyes against the threat of tears, then Dylan would take her in his arms right now and make love to her and make her feel cherished and chase away the loneliness that haunted her heart.

"Let's see if it's working," he said, gently turning Alaina onto her back and combing her hair back from her eyes.

She was beautiful. He didn't bother to wonder

whether it was the Crystal or the allergy medication that had done the trick, but the swelling in her face had reduced to a slight fullness that merely softened the angles. Her eyes were closed, revealing a tracery of fine blue veins in the delicate skin of her lids. Tears clung to her lashes, turning them to soft, dew-kissed black spikes against her cheeks. Her lips were full and red and trembling ever so slightly, like rosebuds in the wind.

All her barriers were gone. Her shields were down. The ice, the polish, the sarcasm, had all fled. She was completely defenseless in this moment as he stared at her. A shiver coursed through him at the realization that this was the woman the bedroom had told him about. This was the woman who hid her fragility from a world that must have hurt her more than once.

Tracing his hand along the porcelain oval of her face, Dylan felt his own defenses drop. In this still, quiet moment of revelation, he opened his heart and fell in love.

Slowly he lowered his mouth to Alaina's, brushing his lips across hers with exquisite care. When she offered no protest, he tasted her again.

She was satin and warmth and a taste like wine, and he thought he would never get enough of her.

Alaina didn't question his kiss, she accepted it. She let her lips part at the request of his and welcomed him into her mouth. Still clutching the Crystal in her fist, she slid her arms around Dylan's neck and pulled him down to her, needing nothing in this instant so much as to hold him. She savored every nuance of the moment—the feel of his muscles beneath her hands, the tingling in her breasts as his chest pressed against them, the gentle thrust of his tongue against hers, the growing ache of need deep in her belly.

A sigh whispered through her lips as Dylan trailed the kiss across the line of her jaw and downward to the smooth, cool column of her throat. She turned her head to allow him better access to the sensitive spot.

This was bliss, to have him touching her this way. Whatever else it might have been didn't matter now. All that mattered was the mutual feeling flowing between them, the need to touch, to communicate in a way that had nothing to do with words or logic. It was as if their souls spoke to each other. Their needs reached out to entwine around each other.

The light that filtered through the window gilded them in tones of gold and sepia. It was that time when day hung on to its last moment before sliding into night, when time seemed suspended in the last rays of the sun. And it was the kind of moment Alaina knew would become suspended in her memory, unrelated to anything that had happened to her before or would happen after.

Dylan raised up, his dark gaze intent as he looked down at Alaina. She met his stare, her blue eyes warm with a certainty that went soul deep. With one hand she tugged loose the belt of her robe and let the garment fall open. Desire swirled through Dylan, robbing him of whatever sanity he may have had left as he feasted his eyes on womanly beauty.

The dress she'd been wearing the night they met had hinted at this. Dylan had imagined the hidden details more than once, but the reality took his breath away. She was every dream he'd ever dreamed. Her large, ripe breasts strained to be free of the mauve lace bra she wore. Her waist was slender, her hips perfectly curved. French-cut mauve lace panties only accented her feminine lines. Beneath them hid her womanly secrets, and below them stretched the shapely legs he had longed to touch, longed to feel wrapped around his hips.

Her invitation was unmistakable. Dylan accepted without hesitation or question. He loved her. Caution kept him from voicing the words. Love wasn't what they had agreed to. In fact, they had both stated it was something they wanted to avoid. Just because his own mind had changed didn't mean Alaina's had...yet. So he wouldn't frighten her by telling her of the feelings that had snuck up and hit him like a freight train, but he would sure as hell show her. Where they would go from there, he didn't know; his impulsive nature wasn't given to thinking far beyond the moment. The important thing was this was right.

Slowly he lifted a hand to Alaina's breast, tracing his fingertips along the scalloped edge of her bra, then slipping them inside to lift the full globe out. As he had imagined, she was warm and heavy in his hand.

Alaina watched him, her breathing shallow, as he bent his head and touched his lips to her nipple. A shudder passed through her when he took the distended peak into his mouth and sucked deeply. She moved restlessly beneath him, anticipation singing along hypersensitive nerves just beneath the fevered surface of her skin.

Her fingers tangled in the unruly curls of his chestnut hair, then roamed to drag his T-shirt up his back. More than her next breath she wanted to feel his skin against hers. As she removed that barrier, Dylan's hand swept down her belly to catch at her panties. His thumb hooked beneath the waistband and dragged the garment down. Alaina lifted her hips to accommodate their descent, gasping as Dylan's thumb delved between feminine petals of flesh to rub against the most sensitive part of her.

Need exploded within her like fireworks, sparkling and brilliant. This was like nothing she had ever known or imagined. Her usual need for control over her passions was vaporized by the heat of this more basic need, the need to come together with this man, only with this man.

She pulled his shirt off and flung it, not noticing or caring that it landed on the window seat and sent her cat running for cover. All her attention was focused on Dylan and the incredible sensations he was conjuring up inside her. She ran her hands over the long muscles of his back, reveling in the tension she found there. He was trembling with desire just as she was. The knowledge gave her a feeling of power and wonder and kinship with him. It was a feeling she shared with him in her kiss when he returned his lips to hers.

While he plundered her mouth, she explored his body. Her fingertips traced over the ridges of his chest, testing the softness of the dark curls there, then following the line of hair to the silky patch that spread across his quivering belly. Without the slightest hesitation her hand slid lower, popping open the button on his jeans and tugging down the zipper that was strained by the evidence of his passion. A groan of carnal satisfaction rolled up from deep in his chest as her fingers slipped his briefs down and closed gently around his shaft. He was hot and full in her hand, throbbing with a need that echoed in her own body, a need that cried out in them both as they stroked each other.

Dylan pulled away from her for just a moment, just long enough to shed the last of his clothes. When he returned, there was nothing between them but desire. Alaina offered herself to him, offered her love, though the words never passed her lips. Dylan hadn't asked for love from her, but she would give it now, silently, because her heart was overflowing with it.

She took him into her body, a soft moan parting her lips as he entered her and sank as deep as he could. Dylan braced himself above her, watching her face as the tightness of her rippled around him, adjusting to his intrusion. She was like hot silk embracing the most masculine part of him. Then her legs were embracing him as well, winding around him as he had dreamed they would, smooth and strong around his lean hips.

He raised one hand to touch her cheek, to brush his thumb across her swollen lower lip, to caress the tip of her dusky nipple that was still wet from his mouth. He drew his hand lower, over the downy softness of her belly to the tangle of dark curls at the juncture of her thighs, and he touched her as he had before—his thumb seeking out the hidden bud. As he caressed her she moved restlessly beneath him and around him.

The only word spoken was his name, whispered softly when Alaina opened her eyes and reached up to him. Dylan lowered himself into her arms, and she held him for a long moment before passion swept them both into a whirlwind.

They moved frantically then, reaching for something they both knew instinctively had been beyond their grasp before. Dylan's movements were strong and rhythmic. He drove deep, trying to give Alaina all the pleasure he could. Alaina clutched at him, lifting her hips into his, digging her fingernails into the straining muscles of his back. They rolled across the bed, tangling in the coverlet. Pillows flew in every direction. The bed creaked beneath them as they sought leverage and angles that rewarded them with sensations unlike any they'd ever known.

So this was what it was like, Alaina thought dimly as the pleasure crested on a wave that took her breath away and filled her with rapture. This was what it was like to make love. This was what it was like to be in love.

It was an emotion she had doubted and derided, feared in a way because it had never really touched her life. It was touching her life now. For one brilliant moment she knew a completion of body and soul that transcended words. As Dylan groaned and stiffened against her, finding his own release, Alaina held him and wondered how she had managed to live this long without him.

And when he left her body, the cold emptiness that filled her made her wonder how she would live beyond this moment.

She was in love with Dylan Harrison, but that had definitely *not* been part of the deal.

Chapter 7

"The deal is off," Alaina said decisively. "I think you'll have to agree with me when I say it simply isn't working out. Eventually our friends will see through the ruse, and we'll have to deal with them. I see no point in delaying the inevitable, do you?"

Her reflection didn't answer her. She stared at herself in the mirror above the sink in her tiny office bathroom, imagining Dylan nodding in agreement, looking grave but sensible.

"Of course he'll agree," she muttered as she leaned toward the mirror, studying her hair with a critical eye. She reached up and yanked out a gray one. "Just because we had fantastic sex doesn't mean he'll be blind to reason."

Her fingers sought out another silver thread among the brown and snatched it out with a practiced flick of the wrist.

Butterflies executed a wild barrel roll in her stomach. She hoped to God Dylan would see reason. After he'd gone home she had sat up in bed most of the night thinking and had come to the conclusion that she didn't want to keep up the pretense of feeling nothing for him when she was feeling something very special and he was not.

For a few moments she had allowed herself the luxury of thinking it might work out between them. She had pictured herself as Dylan's wife, as the mother of his children. In this picture they had been a happy, loving family. It was a nice picture, one she yearned for and feared to reach out for all at once.

"Too good to be true, that's what it is," she muttered, fighting down the ache of tears in her throat.

She had been a fool to let her feelings run away with her the way they had. Really, she couldn't quite understand what had gone wrong. Her emotions never ran as close to the surface as they had yesterday. It wasn't at all normal for her to go around openly yearning for a husband and children. In fact, she seldom allowed herself to think such thoughts at all.

"Must be PMS," she grumbled, pulling out another gray hair.

It wasn't prudent for her to be in love with Dylan Harrison, so she just wouldn't be. Simple. All she had to do was call him and tell him the deal was off.

"No sweat," she said, sounding far more certain than she felt. "I got an A-plus in confrontation."

A sharp knock sounded on the door, and it was pulled open before Alaina had a chance to say anything. Marlene filled the doorway, half-glasses sliding down her nose, a load of mail and paperwork cradled on one flabby arm. "Quit pulling out the gray ones, you'll go bald."

Alaina planted her hands on her hips, outraged at the intrusion and embarrassed at being caught. "Is no part of my life private from you, Marlene?"

"I doubt it. I'm clairvoyant, you know."

Grinding her teeth, Alaina stepped into her office and went to sit behind her table to page through a stack of papers. "So you've told me. Well, if you're reading my mind now, you'll know you'd better have something valid to say, and then you'd better run like hell because I'm contemplating the relative merits of homicide."

Marlene ignored the warning. She shuffled toward the desk, browsing through the mail. "You got an invitation to the California Bar Association annual bash in San Francisco. They want to know if you're going and who you're going with. What do you want me to tell them?"

The Bar Association dinner dance. Alaina stared down at the page in front of her, not seeing a word of the print. How many times in the last few days had she pictured herself attending the gala on Dylan's arm, Dylan decked out in a tux and herself wearing a fabulous, though appropriately understated, dress, the two of them whirling around the dance floor. It was a silly thing, really, but the thought of missing out on that depressed her nearly to the point of tears.

"I know this podiatrist in Gualala," said Marlene.

"I don't need a podiatrist."

"You need a date. He doesn't mind lawyers, though he stated on his match application he would prefer a pedicurist. Interesting guy. He's got an extra little toe on his left foot. Has to have all his shoes custom-made. I'll call him—"

Alaina grimaced. "Over my dead body!"

Marlene waved a hand in dismissal as she moved toward the door. "You'll thank me for it."

"I'll thank you to mind your own business, Marlene," Alaina said tartly. She held out a hand. "Leave the invitation with me; I'll take care of it myself."

"If you take Dylan, you'll have to put him on a leash. He can't stand lawyers—present company excluded, of course," she said, her grating voice lacking the proper enthusiasm.

Alaina's stomach sank like a lead weight. She took the engraved invitation from her secretary's hand and stared at it. Maybe she'd just skip the damn thing. Once upon a time events like the gala had been important to her. It had seemed essential to see and be seen in a crowd of that caliber. It was the kind of atmosphere where contacts were made, where sharp talent jockeyed for position to climb up the ladder of success. Her ambition for such things had gone out. The only reason she had wanted to attend was to go dancing with Dylan.

She swore under her breath. What was this sudden thing she had for dancing? Dancing! Silly, romantic nonsense.

Heaving a sigh, she pushed the thoughts away and cloaked herself in cool professionalism as she looked up at her secretary. "What do I have scheduled for today?"

"You've got a prospective client coming in at ten-thirty about a civil suit." Marlene made her Deputy Skreawupp face and shook her head. "You're not going to like him; he's an Aries."

"Marlene!" Alaina groaned as she lifted her hands to rub at the dull ache that had settled in her temples. "Say you didn't ask him!"

The woman shrugged a heavy shoulder. "It came up in the conversation."

Not trusting herself to say another word, Alaina waved her secretary away. When the door to the outer office clicked shut, she picked up the telephone receiver and dialed Dylan's number.

"Moose Lodge," A cheery voice answered, "Bullwinkle speaking."

Alaina gave the phone a wary look as if it must have goofed up the number itself. Hesitantly she said, "Dylan?"

"Alaina?"

A heavy silence weighed the line between them. On his end, Dylan sat at his worktable in his underwear, enjoying Mrs. Pepoon's day off, which also happened to be his own day off. The kids had left for school with their usual Monday-morning commotion. His intentions had been to spend the morning working on the model of the shuttle craft *Galileo* he and Sam were going to add to their Star Trek collection. The half-finished model lay before him like an open clam shell, waiting. So far he had spent his time eating Oreos and wondering what to do about Alaina.

He was in love with her. It scared him more than a little bit, and he had a feeling she wouldn't be too wild to hear the news herself. She had been drifting off to sleep when he'd slipped out of bed and gotten dressed. He'd left her with a kiss and a promise to call in the morning. Now she'd beaten him to it, and he still hadn't figured out what to say or do.

"How are you feeling?" he asked, hoping he would come up with a strategy by the time she finished answering.

"Fine."

Damn. He hadn't counted on her being stingy with words; she was a lawyer, after all. He passed a hand over his tangled hair and cleared his throat. Alaina cut him off at the pass before he managed to form a thought.

"Listen, Dylan, the reason I called is—ah—I think it would be best if we called the deal off."

All the air left his lungs in a rush. His jaw dropped. "What?"

"It's not working out the way I thought it would, and—um—" Smooth, Alaina, real smooth. Where was that levelheaded woman she had faced in the mirror? Where was that calm, nerves-of-steel woman who had mowed down opposing attorneys and torn their witnesses' testimony to shreds in the courtroom? Elsewhere.

While she hemmed and hawed and stuttered, she picked up a pen and quickly jotted down every reason she shouldn't go on seeing Dylan, leaving off the only one that mattered—she was afraid of getting her heart broken. A huge lump swelled in her throat, and just as quickly, she crossed all the reasons off. She wasn't going to get through them without choking on them, so what was the point?

"Alaina," Dylan murmured, staring blankly at his plate of Oreos. "I don't understand. I thought everything was going really well."

"Right." She gave a derisive half-laugh. "So far I've managed to make a fool of myself, alienate your friends and children, and inflate to twice my normal size. Things are going just peachy, Dylan."

"Well, aside from those...minor incidents..." He winced. No woman considered swelling to twice her normal size a minor incident. New tack, Harrison. "After last night—"

"I don't want to talk about last night," Alaina said, panic slamming into her full force. "To borrow a phrase from you, last night was an accident."

Lord, how it hurt to hear those words, even from her own lips. Making love with Dylan hadn't been accidental. It had been wonderful. It had been special. Too special.

"Look," she whispered because she didn't trust her voice. "I just think it would be best if we didn't see each other anymore."

It took her a split second to realize the soft gasp she'd heard hadn't come from Dylan. Her eyes rounded in horror then narrowed in fury.

"Dammit, Marlene, are you listening?" she demanded.

The silence that answered her question was absolute. Maybe she was just being paranoid. Maybe she had made the sound herself. Maybe she was losing her marbles.

Dylan heaved a sigh. "Princess, don't you think we should talk about this? So there were a few unforeseen glitches in the plan. We can work it out."

He sounded so sincere, so sweet. She couldn't help but think of how tender he had been last night, what a good friend, what a wonderful lover. But it had all been part of the deal for Dylan. No, they couldn't work that out. "I don't think so," she said, just managing to get past the tears in her throat. "I've got a client coming. I have to go now. Good-bye, Dylan."

Dylan stared at the dead receiver in his hand and swore under his breath. He couldn't let her do this. Alaina Montgomery had stolen his heart. Now she was trying to give it back to him. He couldn't let her get away with it.

So making love with him had been an accident? The hell it had. Her invitation the previous night had been very clear, as clear as the panic that had edged her voice throughout her call. She was running scared. From what? A relationship? A guy with a bar and bait shop? A ready-made family? Love? He wasn't sure. He'd never be sure if he let Alaina end it here and now.

With questions and ideas swirling through his head like a Martian dust storm, he slid off his stool and headed down the hall in search of his pants.

"Let me get this straight, Mr. Perkins," Alaina said, sitting back in her chair to level a cool stare at the man who sat on the other side of her desk.

He was in his midforties with thinning brown hair, a thinner mustache, and a fat white brace around his neck. "You went onto your neighbor's private property, climbed onto the roof of his porch to look through his telescope—which he had expressly forbidden you to touch—and you subsequently fell off the roof, injuring your neck."

"That's right."

"And you think you should sue him for how much?"

"One point two million," he said with a perfectly straight face. "What do you think?"

Alaina stared at him for a full half-minute before she could rein in her temper enough to trust her tongue. She rose from her chair and smoothed her hands over the skirt of her gray plaid suit. "I think, Mr. Perkins, that you are an insufferable little money-grubbing ferret." She went on smoothly, calmly, ignoring the alarming color flushing Mr. Perkins's face above his padded collar. "I think, Mr. Perkins, that you ought to be thoroughly ashamed of yourself. You willingly went onto your neighbors' property and injured yourself while abusing their possessions to say nothing of their privacy."

Perkins sputtered as if his neck brace were strangling him. He vaulted out of his chair and shook a finger at Alaina. "They—they—*lured* me over there, having that telescope on the roof and a ladder standing right there! This never would have happened if—"

"—you had minded your own business."

The man gasped in outrage at the suggestion.

The look Alaina gave him was one of utter disdain. "There are few things more offensive to me than someone who chooses to abuse the legal system rather than face up to taking responsibility for their own actions."

Unable to refute the charge, Perkins glared at her as if she had somehow betrayed him. "I thought you were supposed to be some kind of hotshot lawyer from Chicago."

Alaina pulled off the black-rimmed glasses she wore mostly for effect and fixed her would-be client with her iciest stare. "I am some kind of hotshot lawyer, Mr. Perkins. And if I hear you've

tried to pursue this intolerable suit, I will personally see to it that you're found guilty of gross societal malfeasance and negligent hooliganism."

Perkins paled to the color of chalk.

A nasty little smile lifted one corner of Alaina's
mouth as she motioned toward the door. "I think
you can find your way out."

She gave herself a mental pat on the back as
she took her seat once again. How long had she
been wanting to do that? A year, at least. She
would never have been able to tell off a client
when she'd been at Abercrombie. Either she
would have taken the case or one of the junior
sharks circling around her would have. The man's
claim of rights to damages appalled her, but she
knew he could not only get the case to court, he
could probably win it as well, and his poor neighbors would be paying him off for the rest of their
lives.

She may have been short a client, but she had
just gained a large dose of integrity. It felt good.

"Gross societal malfeasance?"

Alaina's heart bounded against her ribs at the
sound of that low, rich voice. She whirled her

chair around to watch Dylan stroll into her office. His hands were tucked into the pockets of his jeans, stretching the fabric across his groin. The faded denim shirt he wore was open at the throat, giving her a glimpse of his chest. He was tan, trim, and fit, with a brilliant symmetrical smile and several unruly chestnut curls trailing across his forehead. All in all, he looked too sexy for words. Alaina's mouth went dry at the sight of him.

She'd missed him. It had been all of—what?—fifteen hours since they'd lain entwined in her bed, naked and warm, replete from making love. And she'd missed him. She literally ached now to have him hold her.

Tamping down her emotions, she shuffled some papers in front of her and said, "It was the first thing that popped into my mind."

"Is there such a charge?"

"No, but Mr. Perkins doesn't know that."

Dylan grinned. From the first he had believed Alaina to be a dyed-in-the-wool materialist. The BMW, the designer-label wardrobe, and all the other trappings of yuppiehood indicated a woman who valued a dollar, perhaps too much. But she had just turned down a chance at a sizable chunk of money, and her reasons had been clear—she had scruples. He had listened to the entire exchange from the other side of the door, which Marlene had conveniently left ajar. It made him feel a lot better knowing he had fallen in love with a woman of integrity.

He gave her office a casual look, taking in the leather-bound books, the diplomas, the handsome upholstered chairs and textured blinds, the Andrew Wyeth lithograph on the wall. Finally he turned back to Alaina. "Quietly pretentious," he said in a teasing tone. "It's you."

Alaina frowned at him, in no mood for his little digs about her expensive tastes. "I happen to like nice things. I don't think that's a crime in this country."

"Crime?" Dylan said with a snort. "It's practically a religion."

Alaina arched a brow. "Is that a fact, Mr. Thirty-foot-fishing-boat?"

Dylan opened his mouth to protest, then clamped it shut and scowled.

Her shot couldn't have been more on target,

but Alaina was too depressed to enjoy the victory. It hurt to see Dylan and know he was no longer going to be a part of her life. She told herself the best thing would simply be never to see him again. The very idea gave her a chill.

"If you came here for a reason," she said in her clipped, businesslike manner as she slipped her glasses back in place, using them like a shield, "I suggest you get to it. I have appointments all day."

"No, you don't." Dylan gave her a smug smile. "You don't have another appointment until tomorrow. Marlene told me."

"How accommodating of her."

"She also told me to tell you she had to leave because she's doing Arlis Cantmorth's astrological charts today. She'll be back at one. And, let's see..." He dug several scraps of notepaper out of his pants pocket and held them at arm's length because he hadn't brought his reading glasses with him. "George Barlow wants to draw up a new will. He's on the outs with his nephew again and wants to leave everything to his Welsh corgi. The copy machine repair people will be here Thursday— I couldn't pin them down as to Thursday of what week of what month. They did, however, promise it would be this year. And the Myerson's Cleaners called to say they *can* get mayonnaise stains out of linen."

Alaina gave him an incredulous look. "You've been out there playing secretary?"

"Yep." Dylan leaned across the table and waggled his eyebrows. "Want to chase me around the desk, boss?"

She scowled at him, but the look that had made lesser men turn tail and run merely bounced off Dylan.

"Oh, yeah," he said cheerfully. "Jayne called. We had a nice chat. She canceled lunch, so I guess that means you're free to go with me."

His grin was too damn tempting. There was a part of her that wanted nothing more than to go with him—anywhere. But on that path lay heartache, and Alaina was not in the market for that. "I'm not going anywhere with you."

Dylan perched a hip on the sturdy table and crossed his arms over his chest, settling in for the battle. "Why not?"

Alaina glanced away from the intensity of his

dark gaze. "We discussed this already. I told you, I don't think the plan is working."

"And I repeat—why not? So things weren't exactly smooth sailing our first time out. We'll work the kinks out as we go. Unless, of course, you're really partial to kinks." That caught her attention. She gave him one of her imperious looks and he grinned unrepentantly. "Handcuffs are okay, but I draw the line at whips." He leaned across the desk again and added in a hotly suggestive tone, "Unless they're made of velvet."

Alaina blushed burgundy and gasped. "You're outrageous!"

"Thoroughly," he agreed. "But am I out in the cold? What do you say, Princess? Is the deal still on?"

She backed away from the issue, literally, pushing her chair back from the desk. "I told you, Dylan. I don't think it's a good idea."

"You thought it was a good idea to begin with."

"That was different. That was before—" She cut herself off, trying to escape the issue further by standing and pacing back and forth behind the table.

"Before we made love?" Dylan suggested softly.

Before I fell in love with you, she corrected him mentally, but wild horses couldn't have dragged the words from her mouth. She stalked back and forth behind the table, her arms crossed before her in symbolic defense. How had she gotten into this mess? she wondered. With one notable exception she had managed to avoid this kind of emotional entanglement for most of her adult life. She'd been right all along in thinking it brought more pain than it was worth. She really had to wonder how her mother did it, leaping from one relationship to the next with barely a pause to catch her breath.

Dylan watched her pace. He watched the emotions that chased across her face. He was right. Alaina was afraid of something. She would no doubt deny it to the death, but she was afraid. He couldn't blame her. He was having his share of nerves too. They had gone into this little game knowing exactly what to expect, but the rules had changed abruptly. He felt as though the ground were shifting beneath his feet. The only thing he was really sure of was that he needed to tread carefully. He needed time with Alaina to find out just where their hearts were headed. He wouldn't get that time if she bolted and ran now.

He circled around behind the table, trapping Alaina in the corner. "This is about last night, isn't it?" he asked softly. "This is about us making love."

"That's got nothing to do with it," Alaina said automatically. The warm timbre of his voice caressed her as surely as his hands had while he'd shared her bed. The memory made her knees sway. She gave him a defiant look, but her trembling chin ruined the effect.

Dylan resisted the urge to take her in his arms. She looked so valiant and vulnerable, trying to be tough and not quite pulling it off. He couldn't keep from reaching out a hand to cup that stubborn chin of hers. "That's got everything to do with it," he murmured. "Alaina, last night we shared something really wonderful, something we both wanted. There's no reason to run away from that."

"I'm not running away!" She denied the charge

vehemently, thinking she could be a damn good liar when the need arose.

"Then the deal's still on," he said, leaning closer, the scent of her perfume luring him like a siren's song. "The terms have changed a little, that's all. Our pseudorelationship is turning out to be more realistic than we'd planned on. Do you have the guts to see where it takes us, or are you going to be a typical lawyer and try to wriggle out through a loophole?"

Alaina's eyes flashed at the insult. Her heart pounded at the promise in his eyes. She swallowed hard, trying to dislodge the knot of indecision that was wedged in her throat.

Dylan gave her a devilish grin, effectively hiding his own fears. "Come on, Princess. Have you really got anything better to do?"

"I'm teaching myself to play the pan flute," she said dryly. "That takes up a lot of my spare time."

"Oh, yeah? Are you taking some lawyer friend to the big wingding in San Francisco? Or are you going to let Marlene set you up with some guy with a foot fetish and extra toes?"

Alaina shot him a scowl. "How did you know about that?"

"Marlene told me."

"Marlene has a big mouth."

"Whales are diminutive by comparison."

Alaina smiled at that, and Dylan brought his thumb up to brush against the corner of her mouth, suddenly wanting her more than he wanted his next breath. They both sobered as awareness wrapped its silken threads around them.

"What do you say, Princess?"

She stared up at him, her heart fluttering in her throat. He was asking her to take a chance, but he was admitting he was taking one as well. They were both well aware of the pitfalls. Knowing all that, what could go wrong? *I could get my heart broken,* she thought. But as she gazed up into Dylan's eyes and remembered all his tenderness of the night before, she couldn't help but think it would be worth the risk to have him hold her again. Hell, she was already in love with him. How could it get any worse?

"I say it's a deal," she said, her voice soft and low.

All the vital organs that had stilled inside Dylan as he had awaited her answer began functioning again. The smile that lit his eyes and canted the corners of his mouth was light with relief as he leaned a little closer. "Good," he whispered, wetting his lips with the tip of his tongue. "In the absence of a notary, we'll seal it with a kiss."

Alaina lifted her mouth to meet his, welcoming the touch and taste of him greedily. It was like taking the first drink after a long period of abstinence. Dylan was no less enthusiastic. He had meant for the kiss to be short and sweet, but the instant he tasted her, his control went up in a blaze of passion. He kissed her rapaciously, his mouth plundering as he pulled her into his arms and molded her feminine form to the hard lines of his own body.

Alaina pressed her hands to his lean cheeks, purring her approval at the day's growth of beard that rubbed against her palms. She might have fussed about his lack of concern for appearances, but the truth was she liked him a little rough and rumpled; it only added to his sexiness. As if he didn't have enough to begin with, she thought as she arched her body into his, coming into delicious contact with the hard ridge of his manhood. To think she had been ready to deprive herself of the wonderful pleasure she'd found in this man's arms. What an idiot, she thought as her hormones took charge of her brain.

"Alaina," Dylan said breathlessly, dragging his lips across her cheek to the shell of her ear, "if we—don't—stop now ..." His sentence was punctuated by pauses made to nibble at the ruby stud in her earlobe. "I won't—be able to."

When Alaina made no comment, he drew back a little, cautious but hopeful. "Alaina?"

Blue eyes gazed up at him, dark with desire. She pulled one corner of her lush lower lip between her teeth.

She wanted him like she'd seldom wanted anything. Shivers of mingled fear and anticipation raced over her. She had nearly lost any chance she had with him, had nearly pushed him out of her life. But here he was, in the flesh. They both may have been tentative about testing the waters of a relationship, but there was nothing tentative about the physical need that hummed between them like electricity. She had never been given to wild impulses, particularly of the sexual variety, but when it came to Dylan, the control she had so carefully cultivated all her life went right out the window, and all that hot blood she'd inherited from Helene came sizzling to the surface.

"The blinds are closed," she whispered, her voice low and hoarse. She stepped back from him and slipped her suit jacket off, tossing it onto her chair.

Dylan never took his eyes off her, but reached up and began unbuttoning his shirt. "I locked the front door when Perkins left."

Alaina stepped out of her pumps and popped the gold cuff links from the sleeves of her white blouse. "Marlene won't be back until one."

Dylan shrugged out of his shirt and toed his battered sneakers off, revealing the long, bony feet he wasn't self-conscious about. Leaning back against the sturdy table that was serving duty as a desk, he held his hands out to Alaina and whispered, "Come here."

She stepped closer. Her blouse was untucked and unbuttoned. Dylan slid his thumbs inside the open placket and drew the fabric to the sides. His breath caught in his lungs at the sight of the silk and lace camisole she wore beneath it. It was filmy and French and barely hid the dark rose-colored circles around her nipples. He sighed as he pulled her into his embrace and caressed his own fevered skin with the feel of cool silk while his fingers worked down the zipper of her snug skirt.

"Are you sure about this?" he whispered.

"There are a lot of things I'm not sure about when it comes to us," Alaina admitted, her lips brushing the skin of his throat. "This isn't one of them."

"Thank God."

Smiling, she nuzzled into his warmth, drinking in his clean masculine scent, tasting his skin with a moist trail of kisses across his solid chest. Her fingers traced the ridges and valleys of his back, drawing around to his belly when she reached the waistband of his jeans. She worked the button free as he worked her skirt down over her hips.

"Holy Hannah," Dylan murmured reverently. His gaze fell down Alaina's supple back to her delectably rounded derriere and beyond to the backs of those shapely legs that filled his dreams. She wore stockings rather than panty hose, stockings that were held in place by a trim white garter belt. The panties she wore were mere whispers of lace, designed to drive a man wild at the sight of them.

He turned, holding Alaina against him with his left arm, and cleared the tabletop with one sweep of his right. Lifting her onto the smooth wood surface, he bent and fastened his mouth on her breast, sucking at her through the barrier of silk.

Alaina moaned and arched her back, tangling her fingers in Dylan's dark hair. She let her eyes drift shut and concentrated on the sensation of his tongue rubbing the wet fabric of her camisole back and forth across her nipple. Incredible. Wonderful. Right. So right. She'd never known what it was to crave a man's touch this way. The prospect had always frightened her. But there was no fear in her now, not with Dylan. When he touched her, she wanted to offer him everything she had, everything she was, everything her lonely heart had stored up inside it.

"Dylan, now," she whispered, reaching for him.

He raised his head and stared down at her, his blood surging in his veins at the erotic picture she made, her fair skin against the dark wood of the tabletop, her hair disheveled, her lips full and pouting from his kiss.

"Not yet, Princess," he said. This desire had sprung up between them suddenly, unexpectedly, but Dylan was determined that it would not pass as quickly. He wanted to prolong this for them both, to stretch out the sweet torture of waiting, making their ultimate reward all the more special.

With his hungry gaze fastened on her long right leg, he unsnapped the tab of her garter. He rolled the stocking down an inch at a time, his lips following the descent with a trail of kisses. Down her thigh, across the inner side of her knee, over the swell of her calf, his mouth drew a line of heat and sensation. The stocking floated to the floor like a silken ribbon. Dylan moved to her left leg and repeated the process, ending with a passionate kiss against the arch of her foot that had Alaina writhing in totally unexpected ecstasy. She had never imagined her foot as an erogenous zone. Dylan was proving her wrong, and for once, she didn't mind.

Lulled to complacency by the languid waves of pleasure he sent rolling through her, she lay back against the table, watching through heavy lids as Dylan bent with a wicked smile and kissed her through the lace of her panties. She sucked in a surprised breath, but made no move to stop him from doing it again. Then the scrap of lace was gone, and long, questing fingers gently probed the tender warmth between her thighs, seeking the source of her heat and making the flames burn hotter all at once. Desire coiled inside her like a spring, tighter and tighter with each caress.

The rasp of a zipper being lowered drew her undivided attention. She leaned up on her elbows and watched with undisguised hunger as Dylan hooked his thumbs under the waistband of both jeans and briefs and eased them slowly downward. He was a beautiful man, a well-endowed man, a fully aroused man...and he was all hers.

She reached out to touch the very tip of him, and it was Dylan's turn to suck in a breath. He groaned as her hand closed around him and stroked him, gently tugging him toward her.

"Now, Dylan," she murmured in his ear as she brought him against her own hot, sensitive flesh.

"Now, Princess," he murmured in return, arching his hips into hers.

He entered her as slowly as he could stand to, holding her gaze with his as she accepted him into the tight silken sheath of her womanhood. Their lips met in one tender, clinging kiss. Then control vanished, driven out by need and desire and a love neither dared voice, a love that had taken fragile root in two wary hearts.

Chapter 8

"Can I ask you a question?" Dylan murmured when he had gathered enough strength to lift his head and look down at Alaina's flushed face.

She opened her cool blue eyes and stared up at him, and he actually felt his heart lurch. He was well and truly in love. The idea made his stomach churn. He hadn't planned on falling in love. He especially hadn't planned on falling in love with Alaina. It seemed he hadn't had a choice. The only thing to do now was proceed with extreme caution.

She reached up and brushed her bangs out of

her eyes, then brushed at the dark curls that tumbled across his forehead. "What?"

What? He drew a blank for an instant, so caught up in the confusing whirlpool of his feelings he'd forgotten the question. *Lighten up, Harrison,* he warned himself.

"Why does Alaina Montgomery, yuppie perfectionist extraordinaire, have a table in her impeccably decorated office instead of the latest in executive desks? Not that I'm complaining, mind you," he hastened to add, caressing the polished wood surface with a loving hand. "I've become inordinately fond of this table. In fact, I think maybe we should have it bronzed and set on a pedestal like a work of art. We could call it 'Plateau of Passion.'"

A wry smile tilted Alaina's lips as she decided to follow Dylan's lead—light and easy, let the future take care of itself. "'Dais of Desire.'"

He lowered his head until the tips of their noses touched. "'Table of Titillation,'" he said in his sexiest voice.

"Enough," Alaina declared, wriggling out from under him and sitting up. She tugged down the hem of her rumpled camisole as she slid off the table and started scavenging for her clothes. "I think it's painfully obvious the art world can get along without us."

"Yes," Dylan said gravely, eyeing her fanny as she bent to retrieve her blouse. "I've seen your painting."

Alaina turned and slugged him in the arm, trying not to laugh. She was a horrible painter. What had ever prompted her to think otherwise, she couldn't imagine. Still, a gentleman wouldn't have pointed out the fact. "That's low, Harrison. They laughed at van Gogh, too, you know."

"Yeah, but that was because he was funny looking with only one ear."

"And if he were alive today, Marlene would try to fix me up with him." She shuddered at the thought.

"See, now aren't you glad you decided to hang on to me for a while?"

For a while. His words hit her in an especially sensitive spot. He wanted them to pursue a relationship, but it sounded as if he still thought of it as only a temporary thing, an interesting diversion. Keeping company with sex.

You're not a mind reader or a fortune-teller, Alaina, she told herself as she snapped her cuff links back in place. *Leave that malarkey to Marlene.*

"I'll say," she quipped, forcing her mood up. "At least you have all the right parts."

"In all the right places," he boasted, striking a comically macho pose.

Alaina rolled her eyes as she zipped her skirt. "You're okay for an old geezer. Don't let it go to your head. To answer your question, I don't have a desk because I haven't found one I like yet. I want an antique. Something substantial, yet elegant."

He nodded knowingly. "Quietly pretentious." When she narrowed her eyes and glared at him, he turned his palms up in innocent surrender. "What can I say? It's you, Princess. Can I ask you another question?"

"What?"

He picked up her brass nameplate from the tabletop and tapped a finger to the engraved surface. "What does the *N* stand for, Alaina N. Montgomery? Nicole? Nola?"

"None of your business," she said coolly as she slipped her suit jacket on.

Dylan gave her a sideways look. "I always feel like people who go by their initials are hiding something."

"Like a name they hate."

"Nadine?" He rubbed his chin in thought. "Norma?"

"No way am I telling you."

He sighed in defeat and looked as sad as a lost puppy. "I'm crushed."

Alaina crossed her arms and tilted her head to an angle that hinted at impatience. "Tough."

Dylan grinned suddenly and draped a long arm around her defensively squared shoulders. "I'll let you off. Temporarily. Now put that pretty patrician nose back in joint and let's go desk hunting. There are zillions of little antiques shops around here. I'll be your personal guide."

"What about the bar?"

He waved a hand in dismissal. "It's only money. I'd rather spend the day with you."

Alaina gave him a look.

He gave up with a shrug. "Okay. It's my day off."

"Come on, Mr. Magnanimous," she said, reaching for the half-eaten Gucci handbag Dylan's dog had tried to devour. "Let's go shopping. You owe me a purse."

Shopping was delayed. They drove first to Alaina's house for a quick shower—which turned into a long shower, a kind of aquatic lovemaking marathon, abandoned only when the hot water ran out and they were forced to leave the stall or suffer hypothermia. Then Dylan fixed them sandwiches while Alaina dried her hair, reapplied her makeup, and dressed in smart white chinos and a blue-striped silk and cotton sweater. On impulse, she added the Crystal to her outfit before nodding her approval at her appearance and marching out of the room.

Dylan frowned at her when she entered the kitchen looking as if she'd just stepped out of the pages of *Glamour*. "Don't you own a pair of jeans?"

"No." She smiled as if she were immensely proud of the fact.

He gave her slacks a dubious look. "You're going antique hunting in white pants?"

"Don't worry," she said, nibbling at the corner of a tuna sandwich. "I don't get dirty. It's against my religion."

She was true to her word. They sifted their way through piles of junk, centuries of stuff people had stopped using but refused to throw out. Alaina came out of each shop daintily dusting off her palms, with not so much as a piece of lint on her impractical white pants.

Dylan simply shook his head. Of course Alaina wouldn't get dirty. She was prim and stylish right down to her oxford-style huaraches. She wasn't the type of woman to get dirty. Veronica had been the same way. The mere thought of getting rumpled had given his ex-wife a migraine. Part of her dissatisfaction with motherhood had been her natural aversion to sticky fingerprints and drool on her wardrobe.

Watching Alaina pick her way through the rubble in yet another backyard antiques shop,

Dylan felt a knot of nerves roll around inside his stomach like a golf ball. How would Alaina take to motherhood? She'd said some women didn't take to the role, but had she been talking about her own mother or herself as well? She claimed his kids had avoided her on the *Tardis,* but she hadn't exactly gotten down on the deck to play with them either. Still, he remembered that poignantly wistful look that had come over her when she'd first seen Cori and Sam, and he took hope. The longing in that look was a rare loose thread in the tightly woven fabric of Alaina Montgomery's image. He intended to take hold of that thread and unravel it.

"Last stop," he announced as he turned the Bronco in at Lindquist Antiques. "If Addie doesn't have it, it probably can't be found on this planet. Of course, Addie might not be able to find it herself. She's a little . . . eccentric."

"Everyone you know is eccentric," Alaina said. "Except me." She frowned prettily. "I hope that doesn't make me eccentric by association."

"I wouldn't worry. Alaina . . . Naomi."

She rolled her eyes and opened the truck's door. "No chance, Harrison."

As they strolled up the sidewalk Alaina stared at the house. It looked like something out of a Vincent Price movie: an eerie, enormous, incongruous blend of turrets, gingerbread, and gables painted a putrid, peeling green. The house was perched on a cliff above the bay on the very northern edge of Anastasia, a lonely promontory where the wind seemed to howl incessantly.

"What a creepy place," she muttered, momentarily forgetting she was too levelheaded to be spooked by such things. "I feel like someone's watching us."

"Someone *is* watching us." Dylan nodded toward a narrow window on the first floor where a hand was drawing back the curtain and a pair of eyes peered at them from the interior gloom as they mounted the creaking steps to the porch. "It's Addie."

The woman cracked the door open in much the same manner as she had held the curtain back, peering out at them with a wary look.

"Hello, Addie," Dylan said, sending her his most amicable smile.

"I don't know you," she said flatly. Glancing

over her shoulder, she said, "I don't know this person, Wimsey."

"Dylan Harrison, Addie," Dylan said calmly. "You know me."

"I do? Oh, well." She swung the door open and stared up at him. She was a trim woman in her early sixties with graying blond hair and sharp blue eyes. She wore a printed cotton dress and green rubber garden boots. "Of course I know you," she snapped impatiently.

"I brought a friend. She's shopping for a desk."

"Well, why on earth would you bring her here?"

"Because you sell antique furniture."

Addie turned and shushed her companion. "Yes, Wimsey, I know that. What do think I am, senile?"

Alaina gave Dylan a look. He just shrugged. The door swung open and Addie Lindquist waved them in. She was completely alone.

"And I thought Marlene was weird," Alaina muttered.

The entire first floor of the house was crammed

with old furniture and relics, odd bits of junk the equally odd Addie Lindquist had collected over the years. Room after room was crowded with dusty, moldy tables and chairs, dressers and bureaus. One parlor held nothing but church pews piled like cordwood. A sunroom was wall-to-wall with old birdcages.

Just when she was ready to give up and go home, Alaina stumbled across exactly the piece she had had in mind all along. It was a large walnut partner's desk with brass ormolu handles on the drawers. What made it different from all the others she'd seen was that it was surprisingly feminine in style, with cabriole legs and graceful carved moldings. It was perfect. And the price tag read $91,763.48.

"It's a tad out of my range," she said dryly, showing Dylan the dusty yellow tag. He choked.

"Addie," he said cautiously, "is this negotiable?"

The woman gave the price tag a glance, then shot Dylan and Alaina a shrewd look. "Maybe. What'll you give me?"

"I was thinking more in the line of three hundred," Alaina said, hoping to get it for five hundred, willing to go to six fifty.

"Hmm...well..." Addie rubbed her chin in thought. She scowled over her shoulder and snapped, "Oh, don't be such a piker, Wimsey." Turning back to Alaina, she said, "You can have it for two fifty." A mischievous smile lifted her pale mouth. "Wimsey will help you load it."

Cursing her conscience under her breath, Alaina wrote the check for five hundred and gave Dylan a look that dared him to comment. His smile warmed her like a shower of golden sunshine. He wrapped an arm around her shoulders as Addie wandered off.

"Come on, you tough cookie, you," he said. "I have a feeling Wimsey isn't going to be a whole lot of help loading this thing."

"Are you sure I won't be imposing?" Alaina asked, unable to keep all the nervousness out of her voice as they pulled up in Dylan's driveway. It welled up like floodwaters inside her and seeped through the cracks in her shield of self-assurance.

"It's kind of hard to be an imposition on pizza-and-Kool-Aid night. We call out for the pizza, and our Kool-Aid cellar is well stocked."

"Well . . . if you're sure."

Dylan noted with no small amount of annoyance that Alaina was staring at his house as if she feared there would be a horde of evil demons lurking inside it. "Alaina, you don't have to do this if you don't want to."

But I'll hate you forever if you don't. He didn't say the words, but Alaina could hear the disappointment simmering in his tone. She swallowed a lump of apprehension, and it hit the bottom of her stomach like lead ballast.

It wasn't that she didn't want to spend the evening with Dylan and his children. That wasn't it at all. It was just that the day had turned out so perfect, she was afraid to push her luck.

Spending the afternoon with Dylan had been wonderful in a way she hadn't even imagined. She liked simply being with him. He was fun and irreverent and sexy and romantic. And when it was just the two of them, she could at least pretend they were meant to be together. Bringing his children into the picture and putting the lot of them together in a domestic setting was only going to shine a glaring spotlight on the fact that she was not the kind of woman he wanted to spend the rest of his life with.

The prospect was disheartening. The fear of failing cut straight through her considerable arsenal of defense mechanisms and pierced her heart like a needle.

Dylan waited for a comment, watching her with a fierce frown. Obviously, she thought spending the day with him was fine, going to bed with him was fine, but a seven- and a nine-year-old would put a damper on the fun. Well, they came as a package, and that was all there was to it. Love her or not, he was prepared to call it quits with Alaina if she didn't accept the fact that he was a very devoted father. His children came first; they had to, especially after what he and Veronica had put them through.

Dammit, why did he seem to be magnetically attracted to career women? Alaina had stated time and again she had no interest in marriage or a family. What made him think he could change her mind? Why couldn't he have fallen in love with Betty Crocker?

"I want to." Alaina blurted the words out. She turned toward Dylan, not at all aware that her eyes were round and wide with uncertainty, with the vulnerability that caught so at his heart. "I just don't want to impose."

His heart melting instantly, Dylan leaned across the seat and kissed her softly parted lips, his hand cupping her cheek. "I want you here, Princess." *Forever, if possible,* he added silently as he ran a forefinger over the vee shape of the Crystal she wore pinned above her left breast.

But would Cori and Sam want her here? Alaina wondered, her own finger absently following the path Dylan's had over the pin she wore. That was the question that had her nerves jangling as she climbed down out of the Bronco and started toward the house the Harrisons called home.

It was a nice place. Certainly not the dreary little abode of a man who shunned life's material luxuries. The house was built on the side of a hill, just a block from the marina. It was no more than ten years old, sided—like the bar—in weathered gray cedar, with lots of angles and glass. A wide deck had been built on three sides and was crowded with overflowing planters and outdoor furniture. A large, expensive-looking telescope took up one corner, pointing toward the sky, just waiting for night to fall. Alaina made a mental note of the pricey toy, but made no comment. Her boundless capacity for argument seemed to have deserted her for the time being.

"You'll have to excuse the mess," Dylan said as he let them in. "It's Mrs. Pepoon's day off. Actually," he admitted, making a face, "it looks this way most of the time. She's so nearsighted, she can't see well enough to really clean the place up."

"Why do you keep a housekeeper who doesn't keep house?" Alaina asked, glancing at the hall mirror that was dim with dust and the table that was buried beneath an assortment of junk and mail and newspapers.

"The kids like her."

It was a simple but very telling answer. Alaina

swallowed and tried not to hyperventilate. She had no real experience with kids. Until recently, she'd spent no time with small children at all. When she'd moved to Anastasia, she'd lived with Faith and her little daughter, Lindy, for a few months while helping Faith set up the inn. That had gone well enough, she reminded herself. She and Lindy were buddies. In fact, it had been during that time that she had begun to feel some very real maternal pangs of her own.

Maybe she would get through this evening just fine. Maybe she was worried about nothing. Maybe all she had to do was relax and let her natural instincts take over.

"What's *she* doing here?" Sam blurted out as he burst into the kitchen with Cori at his heels and Scottie bounding around them, a hairy cloud of canine enthusiasm, his doggie toenails clattering on the tile floor.

Alaina winced. She imagined she could hear her heart hurtling toward her feet like a fighter plane that had been hit by enemy fire, the ominous whine howling in her ears. Bracing for the crash, she leaned a little harder into the stained pine cabinets behind her and crossed her arms a little tighter in front of her.

Dylan frowned at his son, reminding himself that tact was not a nine-year-old's strong suit. "Alaina's staying for supper."

"But Dad," the boy said in a loud, urgent whisper, "what if she's allergic to pizza and blows up like a hot-air balloon again?"

Both children turned to regard Alaina with owl eyes, as if they half-expected her to inflate at the mere suggestion. She smiled weakly.

"Are you aware of having any systemic sensitivity to the ingredients of the common pizza?" Sam asked.

Alaina shook her head. "No."

The boy looked distinctly disappointed. Cori glanced up at her brother and mimicked his expression.

"Hey!" Dylan barked the word so that everyone in the room, including the dog, jumped. He dropped to his knees and scooped Cori up in one arm. "Doesn't your old man rate a hug after a long, hard day off?"

The little girl giggled and wound her arms around his neck. He grabbed Sam around the middle, tickling him as he pulled his son close.

"AAAHHH! Look out!" Dylan shouted. "It's the attack of the wild tickle monster, scourge of the planet Trillermitheron! Run for your lives!"

The children shrieked in delight, wriggling in his arms, but not really trying to get away. Scottie bounced around the knot of Harrisons, barking with deafening exuberance.

Alaina watched with a lump in her throat. What a wonderful father Dylan was. He was the kind of parent every child deserved. He was perfectly natural and at ease with his children, loving them openly and unreservedly.

And she was standing off to the side, as usual, separate, apart. She had never been included in a loving family unit like this one, and she had never felt it hurt quite so badly as it did right now. It was the ache of longing, the ache of wanting something so badly, she was almost afraid to reach out for it, because if she did, and she failed, the pain of returning to loneliness would be unbearable.

"I'm imposing," she said, barely recognizing her own voice, it was so hoarse and thick with tears she refused to shed.

Dylan's heart slammed into his ribs when he looked up at her. He'd never seen anyone look so alone. Letting go of Cori and Sam, he went to her, reaching out to take her hand in his. "No, you're not." Glancing back at his kids, he said, "You guys go get changed and meet us in the workshop. We can show Alaina our collection while we're waiting for the pizza man."

Sam and Cori shuffled in the direction of the hall, their solemn gazes riveted to the intertwined hands of the adults. When the children were out of sight, Dylan pulled Alaina toward him. She held back, leaning into the cupboards, afraid that if she went to him and accepted the strength he was offering, her own strength would crumble and dissolve, and she'd be left with nothing but pain in the end.

"Come here, counselor," he murmured.

"Dylan, I don't—"

He silenced her with a finger to her lips. "Typical lawyer," he muttered, dipping his head down toward hers. "You talk too much."

It was the sweetest of kisses. Alaina couldn't help but drink it in. She had so little control where this man was concerned—and none at the moment. In the deepest, most secret part of her soul all she wanted was to have him hold her as he was holding her now, as if he cherished her, as if he wanted her in his life. There was no way she could even try to resist. So she leaned into him, kissing him back with all the fear and longing in her heart. She let herself melt against him and squeezed her eyes so tightly closed, the tears that gathered at the corners could barely escape.

When he lifted his head, he couldn't help but see them, the crystalline drops that sparkled at the outer edges of her exotic ice-blue eyes. But Dylan wisely made no comment on the tears. "The bathroom is down the hall on the right," he said. "The workshop is in the basement. I'll meet you down there."

The best she could manage was a nod. She made a beeline for the bathroom, cursing herself

under her breath. What the hell was the matter
with her? She didn't ever come apart like this—
never ever. It had been years since she'd let her
emotions run away with her this way. Maybe her
hormones were out of balance, she thought as she
repaired her eye makeup. Maybe she wasn't eating enough protein. Maybe she didn't belong here.

The tears sprang up again, ruining the eyeliner
she had just reapplied. She swore a blue streak,
dabbing at the mess with a tissue. With the iron
will she had built up over the years, she wrestled
her suddenly capricious emotions back into their
little compartment inside her, slammed the door,
and locked it. Leaning back against the cluttered
vanity, she lit up a cigarette and puffed on it furiously, waiting impatiently for the nicotine to
soothe her ragged nerves.

She would get through this. She'd survived
four stepfathers, life with her mother, law school,
and pelvic exams. She'd damn well survive an
evening with the Harrisons.

* * *

"...and this is a scale model of Dr. Who's *Tardis*," Sam explained.

Alaina looked the piece over. It was a foot tall, painted royal blue and white with the words PO-LICE BOX in black above what appeared to be a door. She scratched her head and stared a little harder.

"It looks like a phone booth," she commented at last, feeling like an idiot when Dylan's son looked up at her impatiently.

"It *is* a phone booth."

"Alaina isn't very familiar with the Doctor," Dylan said, steering Sam away from the shelves displaying the Dr. Who memorabilia.

The boy gave Alaina an incredulous look, then turned to his sister and rolled his eyes. Cori shrugged and turned her dark eyes up to Alaina with a look of mingled fading hope and disappointment.

"She'll probably know more about the *Star Trek* stuff," Dylan said hopefully.

They moved to yet another cubicle crammed with books and models. Gold, blue, and red uniform tunics hung on a display rack. The centerpiece of the display was the *Enterprise* herself, a plastic spaceship that hung from the ceiling on fine threads of fishing line. The collection was impressive to say the least, and the least was about all Alaina could say since she knew absolutely nothing about science fiction.

Sam lifted a small black-and-gold rectangle that looked to Alaina like a TV remote control. "This is an authentic Federation phaser used in the first thirteen episodes of the show."

"Really? What does it do?"

The boy stared at her in utter disbelief. "It's a weapon used to kill or stun an enemy."

Keeping her composure wrapped tightly around her like a cloak, Alaina arched a dark brow. "Fascinating."

Dylan choked back a laugh, wrapping an arm around her shoulders as Cori and Sam wandered dejectedly away. "You sound just like Mr. Spock," he said with a chuckle.

"Who's Mr. Spock?"

"First officer and science officer of the *Enterprise*. A Vulcan. A very practical, logical, analytical sort of fellow. You'd love him."

"Is he single? He sounds like my kind of guy."

"Naw." Dylan pulled her unyielding form against him and stole a kiss. Rubbing his nose against hers, he said, "Vulcans have sex only once every seven years. Somehow I can't picture the lady I made love with this morning holding out that long."

"No? Well"—she sniffed—"get on my bad side and see what happens."

Dylan's big hands wandered down over her bottom, squeezing her appreciatively. "Princess," he murmured with a heartfelt groan, "you don't have a bad side."

Above them the doorbell sounded, followed by the thunder of little sneakers and shouts of "The pizza man's here!"

Pizza, Alaina decided, was a great common denominator. Just about everyone liked pizza and held their own opinions as to what toppings and crusts were best. Being from Chicago, she had a natural preference for thick crust, which turned out to be Dylan's favorite as well. Cori and Sam preferred thin crust, but they all agreed on pepperoni as the best topping.

The four of them crowded around the kitchen table eating the pizza directly out of the delivery box and drinking cherry Kool-Aid out of glasses with Peanuts characters on them. Cori had insisted Alaina take the glass with Lucy on it. Alaina had accepted, wondering whether it was a compliment or an insult. Dylan was given the glass with Pig-Pen on it, which seemed rather apropos considering the state of his house.

Once the ice was broken, conversation seemed to flow more easily with the children. Alaina felt herself relax by slow degrees. She listened attentively as Sam related the events of his day, going into a lengthy and complex explanation of his project for the science fair. Dylan had told her Sam was in a special program for gifted students, and she didn't wonder why. It was clear even to someone unfamiliar with children that the boy was extremely bright and sophisticated for his age—so bright, in fact, that he decided Alaina probably wouldn't understand the mathematical applications of his idea and changed the subject.

"That's a genuine Crystal of Kalamari pin you have." He started to point, then remembered his manners and pulled his finger back into his fist in a gesture that reminded Alaina of Dylan's reaction on first seeing her pin.

She sent the larger Harrison male a lazy smile. "So your dad tells me. It was a gift from a friend I went to school with."

"Was he anything like the wizard Danathamien?" Sam asked.

"He's probably more like the absentminded professor," Alaina said, thinking of Bryan. She glanced at Cori, who stared up at the prism full of rainbows with wonder in her dark eyes.

"It's pretty," the little girl murmured, nibbling on her lower lip.

Alaina's heart thumped. These were the first words Cori Harrison had spoken directly to her, and they were accompanied by a tiny shy smile. "You can touch it if you want to."

Cori's face lit up. She scrambled up from the seat of her chair, reaching toward Alaina, her eyes glued to her target so that she didn't see the glass of Kool-Aid until it was too late. Everyone watched in horror as the glass seemed to tip in slow motion, cherry-red liquid gushing out of it in a waterfall that splash-landed all over the lap of Alaina's immaculate white slacks.

There was a long second of ominous silence, then a collective gasp from the people seated around the table. Little Cori, a horrified look on her pale face, burst into tears and bolted from the room. Sam sat back and watched Alaina warily. Dylan tipped his chair over as he jumped out of it to grab a dish towel off the kitchen counter.

Words of apology spilled out of his mouth at the same rate the Kool-Aid had spilled out of the glass as he bent over Alaina, dabbing ineffectually at the spreading red stain. "I'm really sorry. She's at that age where she just walks into a room and things tip over. I'll buy you a new pair of pants. Really, Alaina, I'm so sorry."

Alaina was momentarily stunned to silence by the flurry of activity and the range of reactions going on around her. Her main focus, however, was on Cori, who had run off sobbing as if she'd just committed the crime of the century.

"It's all right," she mumbled at Dylan, pushing his hands away. "It's just a pair of slacks. It's no big deal."

"No big deal? Alaina, boric acid can't take out cherry Kool-Aid stains. Nothing on this planet can."

"I don't care," she said, pushing her chair back.

It was Dylan's turn to be stunned to silence. Fussy, meticulous Alaina didn't care that his daughter had just ruined her flawless, undoubtedly expensive white pants? Veronica would have been furious. Veronica would have been shouting down the house. Veronica would have been giving Cori a tongue-lashing.

Alaina was disappearing down the hall without a word.

She tried one door and discovered Sam's room, tried another and found Fibber McGee's closet. She just managed to push the door shut before the avalanche could start. The third door revealed a room of violet and lavender, cloaked in shadows. The furniture was white and gold, the frilly French-provincial style she had favored as a girl. There was a row of shelves filled with storybooks and stuffed toys. A group of dolls occupied the bed. Kneeling beside it, with her face pressed into the flowered spread, was Cori Harrison, sobbing her little heart out.

"Cori?" Alaina questioned softly as she stepped inside the room.

"I'm s-sorry." The apology came muffled and accented with hiccups and sniffles. "I'm s-sorry."

"I know you are, sweetheart," Alaina said, sitting carefully on the edge of the bed.

The nervousness that had made her feel awkward and uncomfortable with Dylan's children melted away to be replaced by empathy and sympathy and a dozen emotions that had been simmering just under the surface. Seeing Cori now was like looking into her own past, her own lonely childhood, and all the times she'd felt as if she had to walk on eggshells around her mother's latest beau. She could remember incidents painfully similar to this one—some accidents, some purposely staged to test the false affections of a prospective stepfather, all of them ending in tears and disappointment. No one had ever come to her room to comfort or console her.

"I r-ruined your p-pretty outfit," Cori sobbed. "I d-didn't m-mean it."

"I know. It was an accident."

The little girl lifted her head and looked up at Alaina. Her face was streaked with tears, her brown eyes glistened with them. The coffee-brown curls around her face were wet and matted down. "Aren't you m-mad at m-me?"

Alaina bit her lip hard to hold back her own tears. She shook her head. In a gesture that suddenly seemed natural to her, she reached out and opened her arms to invite when all her life she'd kept them closed to ward off rejection. Dylan's daughter hesitated only a second before accepting the invitation. Sniffing back the wave of emotion, Alaina wrapped her arms around Cori and hugged her for all she was worth.

Dylan leaned against the doorjamb, watching through the narrow opening between the frame and the door, which had been left ajar. Tears gathered in his eyes, and he felt the final corner of his heart, that little bit he had been holding in reserve, give way. He was well and truly in love with Alaina Montgomery, and just now it didn't seem like a bad thing at all.

Chapter 9

———

"Are lawyers really allowed to dress that way?"

Jayne sat cross-legged on Alaina's sofa, absently folding the pleats in her wildly flowered skirt. An antique straw hat decorated with silk cabbage roses nearly swallowed up her head.

"Once or twice a year we get to take off the pin-stripes and gray flannel," Alaina said as she fastened the latch on her Crystal pin. She assessed her appearance in the mirror above the mantel with a critical eye.

"You look fabulous."

"I'd better for what this dress cost me."

The gown of softly shimmering, clinging red

silk began in a neat bow on her right shoulder, then draped enticingly across her bosom, hugging her slender, shapely figure as it followed her body's curves, nipping in at her waist and stretching snugly over her hips. The skirt was cut at an angle—thigh-high on the right and falling to just below her knee on the left side. The effect was sexy, but very elegant, which was precisely how she felt this evening. She was finally going dancing with Dylan Harrison and all was right with the world.

As she fastened diamond teardrop earrings to her earlobes, she thought back on the week that had passed since she'd had dinner at Dylan's house. It had been a week of self-discovery, of deepening emotions, of moments of love and moments of blind panic. She didn't like having her feelings churning so close to the surface, didn't like the feeling of not being completely in control, but she was gradually becoming more relaxed with the idea of being in love with Dylan. If she had to relinquish some of her control over her emotions, then Dylan was the man to relinquish it to.

Her relationship with Sam and Cori was moving

forward as well, slowly, carefully forward. All of them were holding back a little, a little wary of committing too much of their bruised hearts too soon. But it was progress nevertheless.

Jayne's amazed voice cut into her musings. "Dylan really agreed to put on a tux and take you to this shindig?"

It was on the tip of her tongue to say that it had been part of the deal, but Alaina bit the words back. The structure of the deal had changed to the point that she didn't like to think about the original scheme anymore. She gave her friend a peeved look as she crossed the room to answer the door. "Of course he agreed to take me. Not even Dylan dresses like a bum all of the time."

She swung the door open and her jaw dropped. Dylan stood on her doorstep dressed in his Dr. Who costume, the brown frock coat buttoned up to his throat, the long, multicolored scarf wound around his neck, the hat tipped at a jaunty angle above his eye. He grinned and gave her a wink as he stepped past her and into the living room.

"You look surprised, Princess. You did say formal attire, didn't you?"

"What is this, Harrison?" she demanded through clenched teeth.

"No, Who is this," Dylan corrected her good-naturedly as he dug into his pocket and pulled out his rumpled bag of candy. "We've been through all this before. Jelly Baby?"

Alaina glared at him. "Are you aware that thirty-nine percent of the homicides in this country are committed against men who underdress for social occasions? And I might point out to you, there are blunt instruments in this room crying out to become evidence in a murder trial."

"Time for me to go," Jayne chirped, popping up from the sofa. "I have no desire to witness a crime of passion."

"Why not?" Alaina asked sardonically, circling Dylan like a she-wolf. "You've already been a witness to a crime of *fashion*."

"I told you, you should have taken the podiatrist," Marlene interjected from the open doorway, her mouth turning down in her Deputy Skreawupp frown. "If I've said it once, I've said it a hundred times—the two of you aren't compatible at all."

"Don't you have a séance to go to?" Alaina asked.

A mischievous smile twinkled on Jayne's face. "She's right, Marlene. We'd better go. We don't want to keep those spiritualistic manifestations waiting." She waved to Dylan. "It's been nice knowing you, Dylan."

He grinned as the pair retreated, and Alaina swung the door shut after them. She turned on him, fury burning icy fires in her arctic-blue eyes.

"I can't believe you would do this to me," she said in a low, tight voice. "The Bar Association dinner is the most important social function of the year."

"What a sad commentary on the state of your social life." Dylan frowned, calmly removing his hat and tossing it onto an overstuffed chair. "This is my way of protesting arbitrary dress codes clung to by the snotty upper class."

Alaina's heart wrenched beneath the bodice of her hideously expensive dress. Dylan really did hate her lifestyle—so much so that he would go to this length to demonstrate his feelings. She pressed a hand to her queasy stomach as her suddenly volatile emotions plummeted downward like a faulty elevator. Maybe Marlene was right. Maybe—

"Relax, Princess." Dylan unwound the scarf from around his neck. His own stomach twisted a little at Alaina's overreaction to his joke. He didn't like to think just how important this occasion was to Alaina, because a frightened little voice kept whispering that it was more important to her than he was. It was practically all she'd talked about for a week.

Personally, he hadn't been looking forward to the evening. Getting trussed up in a penguin suit and hobnobbing with a bunch of stuffed shirts wasn't his idea of a good time. Putting on rumpled pants and a sweatshirt and wrestling with his kids was. He wanted that to be Alaina's idea of fun too. The idea of this formal evening of power socializing scared the hell out of him. But he would go through with it. It was part of the deal.

His scarf joined his hat on the rose-colored chair and was followed by the heavy brown coat. Alaina gasped, but no air made it to her brain, and she had to clutch the back of a chair as her head swam.

He was gorgeous. *Handsome* didn't begin to do him justice. Dylan decked out in a tailored black tuxedo was devastating. The white shirt with its pleated front and stylish wing collar set off the healthy tan of his lean face. The perfectly cut jacket accented his broad shoulders. His only real protest to the order for "black tie" nestled against his throat in the form of a neat, narrow red bow tie.

His hair was too long and a diamond stud sparkled in his earlobe, but these features only added to his air of being the charming rake. What woman could resist the bad boy in formal attire? Certainly not her, Alaina mused, weak-kneed beneath her Bill Blass original.

"Typical lawyer," Dylan muttered, stepping close and cupping her bare shoulders with his hands. He bent his head down and brushed his lips lightly across hers. "Can't take a joke."

She gave him a sheepish smile as she slid her palms up the lapels of his jacket and interlaced her fingers behind his neck, twining soft tendrils of his chestnut hair into the union. "Don't you know you should never tease a woman who has recently spent a sum to rival the national debt on a gown from Neiman Marcus?"

Dylan cast a pained look at the ceiling.

Alaina took advantage of the tilt of his chin to press a soft kiss to his throat, then rubbed the smudge of lipstick away with the pad of her thumb. Her eyes were wide and guileless when they met his. "Take me dancing," she whispered.

The joke about lawyers being expert dancers stilled on his tongue as Dylan stared at the woman who stood in the circle of his arms. For one highly charged moment neither of them said anything, but communication of another sort bridged the gap between their souls, between their differences in style and philosophy. For just an instant Alaina was nothing more complicated than the woman he loved.

"How can I say no?" he murmured, his right hand trailing down the cool silk of her bodice to the pin she wore. Almost reverently, his blunt-tipped fingers traced the Crystal. "It's bad luck for a man to deny a woman wearing the Crystal of Kalamari. I'll bet you didn't know you could claim my heart forever or damn my soul for all eternity just by making a wish."

Something vital and fragile trembled deep inside Alaina's heart. If only she believed in such foolishness, she thought. If only love were as simple as making a wish or chasing a rainbow.

Pushing the uncomfortable sense of vulnerability aside, she gave Dylan a subdued version of her sassy look. "And all I wanted was a fox-trot."

Dylan smiled. "Decadently expensive or not, you look gorgeous. I'd love to take you dancing, Alaina... Noreen. Nita? Nancy..."

The ballroom was the height of ostentatious opulence—a soaring ceiling, gaudy gilt trim, a waxed wood floor that shone like polished glass. That floor was a sea of tuxedos and evening gowns. The place was thick with lawyers milling around like so many pricey show horses. After-dinner conversations were about class action suits, out-of-court settlements, golf scores, and foreign cars. They were a long way from Anastasia. This was the world Dylan had left behind.

Money, power, status: the idols he had once wor-
shipped then cast aside in favor of a more meaningful existence. This was the world Veronica had
left him for. This was the world that fit Alaina
Montgomery like a designer gown. She had never
looked so comfortable as she did with a glass of
Dom Pérignon in her hand. She smiled up at the
man they were being introduced to, glowing like a
diamond in a Cartier setting.

Dylan hooked a finger inside the collar of his
shirt and swallowed an enormous knot of apprehension. This was Alaina's element. Why would
she throw it all away for a guy who ran a bar and
bait shop? She'd seemed genuinely happy spending time with him and the kids this past week, but
obviously that wasn't enough for her. Obviously,
she was just biding her time in Anastasia, waiting
for opportunity to knock and invite her into the
big leagues of California law.

"...and this is my friend, Dylan Harrison,"
Alaina said, laying a hand on Dylan's forearm.
"He's involved in several businesses in Anastasia."
The muscles beneath her fingertips tightened to
the consistency of granite.

"Harrison," the beetle-browed icon of San Francisco law mused, pursing his thick lips. "One of the Sacramento Harrisons? Lumber and cattle?"

"No," Dylan said tightly. "One of the Moose Hollow, Oregon, Harrisons. Beer and bait."

The attorney opened his mouth and closed it again in an unconscious imitation of a fish.

"If you'll excuse us," Dylan said, snatching the wineglass out of Alaina's hand and thrusting it onto a passing waiter's tray. "I promised Ms. Montgomery this dance."

Alaina's opinion of his manners was drowned out by her squeal of surprise as Dylan all but hurled her onto the dance floor. Fuming, she settled into his rigid embrace. She *never* squealed. She particularly did not squeal in front of her peers. Digging her neatly manicured nails into Dylan's shoulder, she sent him a scathing look.

"I'm not into slam dancing."

Dylan gave a snort. "Who could be with this music?" Clarinets droned in the background as he rolled his eyes. "Lawrence Welk would be bored to tears at this place."

"What did you expect, Run-D.M.C.?"

"No. The only thing lawyers know about rap is how to beat it when their client is a two-time loser as guilty as sin."

Alaina's anger was tempered by her disappointment. She had hoped this evening would be an enjoyable one. Though she would never admit it in a million years, she had wasted all kinds of time daydreaming about having Dylan sweep her around the dance floor. He seemed more determined to sweep the dance floor with her.

"Look, I know you're having a lousy time," she said. "But you could pretend otherwise. After all, I put up with your picnic. You owe me this; it was part of the deal."

"The deal." He couldn't quite bite back his groan. "Don't remind me."

So now he wished he'd never made the deal. He probably wished he'd never laid eyes on her either, Alaina thought glumly. Well, he had stated from the beginning she wasn't his type. Lord, that idea rankled. Why wasn't she his type? Because she liked nice things? His tastes were no less expensive, just different. Of course, the self-righteous bugger was too blind to see that.

"You know, this would be much more pleasant if you weren't determined· to play the reverse snob," she said as they made their way stiffly around the dance floor to a watered-down version of "Celebration."

"*I'm* a snob?" Lifting his nose with exaggerated hauteur, he looked down at her and spoke in a dry falsetto. "Dylan is involved in several businesses in Anastasia."

"Well," Alaina mumbled, not quite able to look him in the eye, "you are."

"I chose to walk away from all this pretentious baloney, Princess," he said, maneuvering her around a rotund couple doing the rumba. "I'm not ashamed of what I do for a living."

"I'm not ashamed of what you do either. I'm ashamed of how you're behaving."

"Oh, well, I'm sorry." His voice dripped sarcasm. "Us Moose Hollow Harrisons don't know spit about how to behave in polite society. Maybe you should have asked your lumber baron friend, Knute Grabowski, to bring you."

Alaina flashed a smile at a passing couple, then turned to Dylan, hissing fury between her teeth. "Knute Grabowski is not a lumber baron. He's a thickheaded, mannerless..." she began, calling up the memory of her blind date with Jayne's lumberjack friend. She'd never had a more miserable night in her life—until tonight. She shrugged and gave a half laugh. "Come to think of it, aside from the tattoos, I can't see much difference between the two of you."

Dylan gave her an incredulous look that melted into one of introspection. She was right. He was being a pig. Considering his past, he had every right to feel threatened by Alaina's preference for high society, but the way he was behaving was only going to drive her to it, not from it, not into his arms. And she felt too damn good in his arms to let her go, he thought as he pulled her a little closer. What he needed to do was woo her into making their deal to keep company a permanent one, make her see that life with him and his children could be fulfilling in a way haute cuisine and haute couture were not.

He dipped his head down, intending to apologize. Just as he opened his mouth, Alaina turned abruptly away, smacking him in the teeth with her dangling diamond earring.

"Skip Whittaker!" she exclaimed in surprise, stepping out of Dylan's arms and off the dance floor to greet her old friend from law school.

Whittaker looked as if he'd been born wearing a tuxedo. His limp blond hair was cut fashionably short on the sides, and his smile spoke of wealth and an excellent orthodontist. He greeted Alaina warmly—a little too warmly in Dylan's opinion. Dylan stood awkwardly to one side wincing, scowling, and fingering his teeth for chips.

"Skip, I'd like you to meet my friend, Dylan Harrison." Alaina gave Dylan a meaningful glare and said, "He sells swill and chum on the waterfront."

Whittaker's proper blond brows rose and fell. He gave Dylan a once-over that clearly said Alaina had suffered from a momentary lapse in judgment when choosing her escort. His gaze lingered disdainfully on Dylan's red tie, then Whittaker dismissed him altogether, turning Alaina's way. "I'd heard you left Abercrombie, Turtletaub, and Flinch. What are you doing out here?"

"Starting my own practice in a little town up the coast."

Skip frowned as if the gravlax from the buffet was coming back on him. "Probate and petty theft? You'll be bored to distraction inside six months."

Alaina lifted one shoulder in a delicate, defensive shrug. "Well, we can't all be overpaid corporate sharks like you, Skippy."

Whittaker beamed. "True, darling, but you're one of the best. Your talents are being wasted. You could be pulling down six figures annually, have a Mercedes and a condo in Marin County. I know we would pay dearly to have you at Victor-Ruthton."

"You're with Vicious-Ruthless?" Dylan questioned, horning his way into the conversation with a devilish grin and a demonic light in his eyes. Everything about Whittaker rubbed him the wrong way, from the part in his hair to the slight whine in his voice. And he took particular exception to the way the man was trying to entice Alaina away from Anastasia. Never mind that he had never expected her to stay. He couldn't stand the thought of her being lured away by a pretentious preppy and promises of an overpriced loft. "Why, Chip, I'll bet you know my ex-wife's attorneys— DoWe, Cheatem, and How."

Whittaker choked on his champagne, his eyes rounding behind his fashionable spectacles. Alaina felt all her red blood cells shoot to her feet to hide there in mortification.

"Isn't that funny?" Dylan asked, straight-faced. "I have the same reaction when people mention their names to me too. Why, just the other day I was talking with Goldie Chargecard about the price of Volvos with CD players versus the price of Volvos with cellular phones, when she happened to mention that firm." He gave an elaborate shrug. "I lost my quiche right there and then. All over my Lord and Taylor wingtips. It was tragic, really."

All of Alaina's embarrassment lodged in her throat, and she fell into a coughing fit. Skip had turned an ominous shade of gray, and people around them were beginning to stare. How could Dylan do this to her? More to the point, if she silenced him with a shrimp fork from the nearest table, would she get away with a plea of temporary insanity?

"Kill—kill—" she rasped between coughs, smacking him on the arm with her fist.

"I tell her and tell her to quit smoking," Dylan said, draping an arm around her shoulders. "Cigarettes are so unfashionable, don't you think, Dippy?"

Whittaker scowled. Alaina reached for Dylan's throat. "Die—die—"

He heaved a long, suffering sigh. "I'd better take her outside for some fresh air. It was *sooo* nice meeting you. We'll do lunch."

The air that greeted them outside the hotel was fresh and cool, tinged with the flavor of the sea that drifted up from the bay. Alaina gulped down great breaths of it as she leaned back against the cool stone of the building, trying to get control of herself. In the distance a trolley bell clanged.

Dylan jammed his hands in his pants pockets and let the tension drain from his shoulders. He'd really stuck his foot in it this time, he thought, squeezing his eyes shut against a wave of self-recrimination. He'd ruined Alaina's big evening, made an ass of himself in front of her colleagues. *Great strategy, Harrison, she's going to virtually throw herself at you now.*

"I'm sorry," he said with a long, sad sigh as he fell back against the building. What an inadequate thing to say, he thought. But he found himself caught in a trap of his own making. How could he tell Alaina he felt threatened by the world her lawyer friends represented? How could he tell her he was afraid of losing her when he'd promised to make no claim on her?

"Oh, that's okay," she said sardonically. "You only ruined my standing in the legal community and shot to hell any chance I ever had of gaining prominence here. It's nothing, really; just my career."

And her career was important to her. Prestige was important to her. Dylan felt his heart sinking. He should have seen this coming.

"Marlene was right," Alaina went on as she dipped into her silk evening bag for a cigarette. "I should have brought you on a leash. Or I should have brought the podiatrist. The worst he could have done was discuss hammertoes and plantar warts at the dinner table."

"I'll make it up to you."

"Please don't. I wouldn't want the guilt associated with orphaning your children." She watched the stream of smoke she exhaled toward the moon, a wistful expression falling over her elegant features. "I didn't even get to dance a whole song."

Dylan leaned close, one hand reaching up to brush at her stylish dark hair. Maybe they didn't belong together. Maybe they couldn't make it work. Maybe those thoughts hurt like hell. But a deal was a deal. He owed her. And the idea of holding her close was one he wasn't ready to let go of just yet.

"Come on, Princess," he said, taking her free hand and pulling her away from the wall. "Let me take you dancing."

"I'm no expert," Alaina said when she slid out of the car and looked around, "but this looks like a marina."

"It *is* a marina." Dylan dug in his pocket for a set of keys, then offered Alaina his hand and led the way across the parking lot toward a gate. "Welcome to Sausalito. If you'll recall, you left the choice of accommodations for this evening up to me."

"I recall," Alaina said without enthusiasm. "Heaven only knows what possessed me." She stared past him as he paused to unlock the gate that barred the dock. "If you think you're going to take me out on a boat, I'll tell you right now—I'll throw up. And if I throw up on this dress, your tab is going to resemble the defense budget."

"I promise we won't leave the marina."

They made their way down the dock, Alaina picking her way along to avoid sticking a heel between the rough boards. Her attention was divided between her progress down the pier and the structures that nestled side by side in the inky water.

"Houseboats," Dylan explained. "There are a couple hundred permanently moored here. People live in them year-round."

They didn't even remotely resemble boats,

Alaina thought. They were, quite literally, small houses built on floating platforms. In the illumination of the security light Alaina could make out their shapes and general details. Some were simple dwellings, others were two stories high and had elaborate decks with latticework balustrades.

"Your barge for the evening, Cleopatra," Dylan said, bowing and waving his arm in a flourish toward the last houseboat in the line.

Alaina gave him a skeptical look. "Mine?"

"Borrowed from a friend who's spending the weekend in L.A. It's a boat that doesn't move. The perfect way for you to get your sea legs."

"I like the legs I have just fine," Alaina said dryly as she took his hand and stepped onto the deck of the houseboat. The porch light spilled across her exposed right thigh as the silk of her skirt slid away, giving Dylan a glimpse of black lace at the top of her stocking.

He heaved a heartfelt sigh. "Me too."

Alaina tapped his cheek. "Chill out, Captain Bligh. You can give me a tour of this tub before you ravish me."

He brightened at that. "I get to ravish you?"

"Only after we're finished dancing."

"You're a soulless tease," he declared dramatically. "A merciless coquette, heartlessly toying with the affections of adoring males."

She gave him a look. "Dancing was the deal, Harrison. Be glad I'm letting you off that easy. I could probably sue you for irretrievably damaging my image."

"You'll bounce back," he said, not quite able to sound snappy. "You're a tough cookie."

The houseboat was small but charming. The main level included a living room that opened onto the deck via French doors. Comfort ruled here with inviting furniture in neutral colors and bright handwoven pillows. The kitchen/dining area boasted oak cupboards, a skylight, and a jungle of hanging plants.

They wound their way up a spiral staircase to the bedroom, which was situated directly over the living room, and like the living room, had French doors that opened onto a deck. As in the kitchen, there was a skylight. But this was no ordinary skylight that was positioned directly over the bed. This one was made of stained glass and poured a rainbow of muted colors on the white goose-down comforter.

Alaina stopped in her tracks and stared at the bed, her heart beating a curious rhythm. Rainbows. When she'd come to California, she'd felt as if she were chasing one. Tonight she would make love beneath one.

Rainbows have lots of magic in them, Bryan Hennessy had once told her. If she dared to believe in that magic for once, would it make a difference? Would it erase the fear she'd felt all evening that Dylan was suddenly slipping away from her, that he was so stubbornly set against the lifestyle she led that he would never want to amend the deal they'd made?

"That dance, Princess?"

Dylan's voice was a velvet caress against the back of her neck. She didn't fight the urge to lean back into his warmth and strength. His arms slid around her waist, binding her to him. She could feel his heartbeat against her back.

"We'll have the floor all to ourselves, and the stars will be our chandeliers," he murmured, his lips brushing the shell of her ear. "Great line, huh?

I got it from a Fred Astaire movie. He and Ginger were shipwrecked on an island—in evening clothes, of course."

"Of course." Alaina turned in his arms and smiled softly up at him. She loved this man. He was the perfect combination of wit and whimsy, practicality and piffle. She only wished she had the nerve to tell him. But after his performance at the hotel, she was more insecure about their future than ever, and so she remained silent.

Leaving the French doors open, they went out onto the deck. The deck was situated so they couldn't see another houseboat, giving Alaina the feeling that they had the harbor all to themselves. To one side of the marina rose the steep hills where the homes of Sausalito clung in a fashion reminiscent of the Italian Riviera. To the other side stretched the starlit waters of the bay. Music from the stereo in the bedroom floated out, soft and dreamy.

It was lovely. It was—dare she think it?—magical.

She gave in to the feeling as Dylan took her in his arms and began swaying to the music. Not even a confirmed nonromantic could resist moon-light and sea breezes and the bluesy wail of a sax-ophone.

The song went on, slowly and effortlessly. Alaina floated with it. She wound her arms around Dylan, wrapped herself around his heart, forgetting for the moment their deal and their dif-ferences. She melted against him, all softness and hope and love unspoken. She even let him lead.

They slow-danced across the gently swaying deck and back again, eventually finding their way through the French doors. Standing beside the color-splashed bed, Alaina reached up and untied Dylan's red bow tie. Her fingers walked down his shirtfront, liberating the white pearl studs from their moorings, opening the crisp fabric to reveal tanned flesh and curling dark hair.

She pressed her lips to his skin, at once kissing him and drinking in his fragrance. The jacket of his tux slipped back off his broad shoulders and whispered to the floor, revealing suspenders that matched his tie. Alaina hooked her thumbs be-neath them and tugged them down to hang in loops from the waistband of his pants.

Her hands roamed to his zipper and eased it down. Gently she stroked the essence of him, cupped him, teased him, finally freeing him from his trousers and pressing him against the smooth, warm silk that covered her belly, all the while lavishing languid kisses across his chest from one flat, brown nipple to the other.

Dylan groaned in mingled pleasure and anticipation. She would be no less warm or silky when she opened herself for him and accepted him inside her. With that knowledge spurring him, he stood back from her and shucked his shoes, socks, and pants. Naked except for the shirt that hung open and the tie that hung like a ribbon around his neck, he sank down on the bed and leaned back against the mound of pillows, his eyes never leaving Alaina.

Feeling as though she were peeling away layers of armor, Alaina lowered the zipper in the side of her dress and bared herself to Dylan's gaze. The silk dress whispered as it slid to her feet, spilling into a pool of color on the white rug, a pillow of red for the Crystal pin that fell in its center.

She stood absolutely still, letting him look his

fill, feeling naked in a way that had nothing to do with clothing. This wasn't just a prelude to sex. This was something more. This was letting go of some final barrier. She had never felt so vulnerable or so unable to shield that vulnerability.

Dylan felt everything inside him still as he looked at her. She was stunning. Her breasts were proud and full with nipples drawn into tight knots at the center of large dusky-rose discs. Her waist tapered then flared gracefully. Sheer dark stockings stretched from her toes to the tops of her thighs, ending in a band of black lace. At the apex of those long legs was the triangle of dark curls that covered her most feminine secrets.

He held his hand out to her and drew her down to the bed so that she sat facing him, her bare hip brushing his thigh.

"If I'd known you were naked under that dress, we never would have made it through dinner," he said in a low, rough voice.

"Silk shows everything, you know," she whispered in a tone so intimate she barely recognized her own voice. "Personally, I would rather sacrifice modesty than be caught with an unsightly panty line."

"I'm not complaining."

One of her shoes hit the rug, then the other. Dylan slid his hands over her shapely calf, under her knee, and up her thigh to the band of her stocking. His fingers trailed upward to just brush her most sensitive flesh, then fell back to peel the silk down her leg.

Alaina leaned back on her hands, sighing her pleasure as he repeated the process with the other leg. Warmth coursed through her. Desire unchecked. She let go of all logical, practical thought. There was no room for it here. Here, now, there was room only for feeling and for expressing that feeling in a way that transcended words.

Dylan reached for her, pulling her toward him with one hand on her shoulder, the other roaming freely over her breast. "I want you, Alaina," he murmured, rubbing his cheek against hers. "I want to feel you hot and wet around me."

Kneeling on the bed, she leaned into him. Her fingers closed around his wrist and she drew his hand downward, across her stomach to the juncture of her thighs, opening herself to his gentle exploration. She moaned as he parted the petals of her flesh and found her moist and ready for him. Any remnant of inhibition that still clung to her fell away as he eased a finger into her at the same instant he slid his tongue into her mouth.

This was what she wanted—to be possessed by this man, to have him fill her in every way; to have him want her—not just as a temporary partner, but as a soul mate, the woman he could share his whole life with. But as badly as she wanted to tell him, as much as her heart ached with need to share her love, she said nothing. A very old, deeply seated fear refused to die with the rest of her defenses, a fear that had been resurrected anew during the course of the evening.

If Dylan decided he didn't want her, couldn't live with her career and her tastes, if he decided to walk away, she would be left alone and lonely, as she had been for most of her life. And she had learned long ago that it hurt less to say good-bye to someone who didn't realize what their leaving was doing to her heart. So she kept the words to herself and gave Dylan her love without promises, neither offering nor asking for ties.

Caressing his face with fingertips that vibrated with sensitivity, she mounted him and took him into the secret silken pocket of her body, embracing the most masculine part of him with the essence of her femininity. With the muted rainbow of light dappling their skin from above, she moved on him until he groaned and arched upward, his completion filling her with warmth.

She squeezed her eyes shut, but the colors stayed with her—beautiful, brilliant colors that tumbled and swirled as her body tightened around Dylan's and shuddered in a climax so powerful, she thought she might lose herself in it completely. When she looked down at Dylan, he was bathed in those colors, a rainbow of magic and love. And she recalled the words she had spoken one day long, long ago, saying that rainbows were nothing more than the diffusion of light through raindrops.

She couldn't have been more wrong. She could see that now. Her logical mind had clung to its reason, protecting her with prosaic practicality.

She had hidden from the beauty of magic by denying its existence. Now she could see it, and it was so wonderful, it took her breath away. But the price of that glimpse of magic was dear. She'd never been so frightened in her life.

Dylan could feel her pulling away—emotionally and physically. Like a treasure chest that had opened to give him a glimpse of the wonderful, beautiful, shining gifts inside, the lid was suddenly dropping so he could see only the exterior, the facade. He raised up on one elbow as Alaina slipped from the bed and bent to pick up the red silk gown she had dropped on the floor. All he could see of the inner woman now was a glimpse of vulnerability in her eyes as she brushed her fingers across the Crystal pin fastened to the dress, and that glimpse was so brief he was afraid he had imagined it.

In fact, it had looked more like regret than anything, he thought, a fist of tension twisting in his gut. What was she thinking? That she wished she had gotten to show off the dress more at the dance? That she would still be there networking with her colleagues, making the proper impression on all the right people, if he hadn't screwed things up and offended everyone within earshot? That she would rather be in the ballroom making points with her peers than in this bedroom making love with the owner of a bar and bait shop?

"Can't that wait?" he asked as he watched her open the louvered door of the closet and rummage through for a decent hanger.

Alaina gave a shrug. "Sorry, darling, but it's like my mother always said: Men come and men go, but a Bill Blass original is timeless. One must treat it with proper respect."

Men come and men go. Dylan frowned and pulled the sheet up a little tighter around his waist. "Sorry you didn't have the chance to show it off more tonight."

"There'll be other occasions—provided you didn't get my name scratched off the A-list for all eternity."

Other occasions, Dylan mused. How many occasions could there be for a small-town attorney to put on a designer gown? Bill Blass didn't get a lot of wear around Anastasia.

You'll be bored to distraction inside six months. All he had to do was close his eyes and he could see Skip Whittaker reciting those words. He could see Alaina glowing beneath the light of crystal chandeliers and hear her sharp-tongued repartee. And he remembered what he'd thought when he'd first met her: that she had come to Anastasia for a change of scenery. There had been no question in his mind that she wouldn't stay. Hell, that was why he had proposed this confounded deal to begin with!

He had tricked himself into believing he could simply keep company with Alaina Montgomery, enjoying her obvious charms without losing his heart. Now his heart was lost and all Alaina seemed to be able to do was remind him their situation wasn't permanent. It was just a deal, a convenience with some great sex thrown in. Six-figure incomes and Bill Blass gowns were her world, not fishing boats and bartenders and schedules that revolved around children.

A cold wave of fear left his skin pebbled with goose bumps. What had he been thinking about, falling in love with Alaina Montgomery? It wasn't only his own heart at stake. He had involved Cori and Sam as well. They had been growing fond of Alaina. What was going to happen to them when she got bored with Anastasia and went back to the bright lights and excitement of the city and big-time law? What would happen when she left them—just as Veronica had?

The old wound opened as if it had simply scarred over but never really healed. He'd never been so frightened in his life.

He stared at Alaina. Alaina stared back. Neither realized the sudden wariness they saw on the other's face was just a reflection of their own expressions. Raw nerves hummed in the still night air. Tender feelings that each had buried lay open and vulnerable, and hearts that longed for love but feared rejection ached half a room apart. And overhead, clouds rolled in to obscure the moon, and the rainbow that had poured down from the skylight vanished into darkness.

Chapter 10

It was the beginning of the end. She could feel it. In a dozen subtle little ways Alaina could feel Dylan pulling back from her. The days of their deal were numbered.

She sat at her newly refinished desk—the desk Dylan had helped her find—mentally going over the checklist of danger signals as she pretended to listen to her client. Her stomach churned as she called to mind all the little digs against her lifestyle and her career he had shot at her in the three days since their trip to San Francisco. Not that he hadn't done that from day one, but there was a difference in his tone these days. There was a definite chill in the air that had little to do with the approach of winter.

To make matters worse, her natural reaction was to fight back. If he picked on her car, she retaliated with remarks about his truck. When he sniped at her preference for designer labels, she lambasted his liking for dilapidated denim and shirts that would make Hawaiians cringe.

They were caught in a horrible downward spiral that was pushing them apart until they seemed like strangers with nothing in common except sexual preferences.

It had all started with that damned dinner dance. Why had she gotten so head up about going dancing with him? Was she developing some kind of fatalistic Ginger Rogers fixation or what? She should have known Dylan would hate anything as vainglorious as a Bar Association social function. Everything about it would rub him the wrong way—including her role. Somewhere between the hors d'oeuvres and the adieus he had come to a decision about her. He didn't want her.

Oh, he'd been able to put up with her short-term, but over the long haul Dylan Harrison didn't want a woman who looked stunning in a Bill Blass gown. He wanted a woman who looked good wearing an apron with cookie dough smeared on it. He wanted a woman who didn't turn green at the mere mention of a boat—ship. Hell, what difference did it make what it was called? It was becoming plain that she wouldn't need to know.

And what about the beautiful love they'd made on the borrowed houseboat? A fond farewell, perhaps. A last good tumble. A memory gilded in the colors of a rainbow.

There was one more date left on the list of events they had agreed to attend together: Dylan's family reunion. After Sunday their contract would be up for renewal, but Alaina had the sinking feeling Dylan wasn't going to pick up the option.

She swallowed at the fist-sized lump that was stuck in her throat. A fine flame of anger burned off the haze of melancholy. Why the hell had she gone and fallen in love with that bar-and-bait-shop buffoon anyway? Hadn't she made up her mind she was better off without love, without a man? She'd seen it happen time and again: Men did nothing but complicate a woman's life.

"He's a royal pain in the patootie," a little voice chirped.

"You've got that right," Alaina grumbled.

"Gee, sweetie," said the blue-haired little old lady seated before the desk. "It's one thing for me to say so. I'm his granny, after all. I'm the one he's barfed on at every major occasion of his life. It's like his genes were programmed by that mother of his. She probably played subliminal messages to him when he was in her womb."

Alaina's brows drew together, and she sat up straighter in her chair as her brain tried to push through the cotton-wool fog of distraction. "Dylan threw up on you?"

"Dylan who?"

"Who? Oh, please," Alaina said with a groan. She rubbed a hand across her forehead. "Don't let's start with the Abbott and Costello thing again. I'm really not up to it."

"Her biorhythms are all out of whack, Mrs. Bostwick," Marlene said, barging into the office. She wore purple leggings and yards and yards of brilliant pink gauze sewn into a garment that looked as if it could have served double duty as a tunic or a circus tent. "Maybe you should come back in a day or two to discuss your grandson's trust fund."

Alaina scowled at her secretary, a Doberman-like snarl rumbling behind her barred teeth. "Marlene..."

Mrs. Bostwick turned in her chair. "You think she'll be better by then?"

Marlene waved a hand glowing with mood rings. "No sweat. Venus will be in Virgo. She'll be in a mental upswing."

"I hope so," Mrs. Bostwick said, pushing her tiny frame up out of the visitor's chair, "because right now I'd have to say she's a bubbleheaded bimbo."

Alaina's spine straightened at the insult. "I beg your pardon?"

"Come back on Monday," Marlene instructed, not sparing her boss so much as a glance. "You'll thank me for it, Hilda."

Steaming with indignation, Alaina watched

her secretary usher the potential client out of her office.

"Marlene, have you ever contemplated what it might be like to stand in the unemployment line?" she asked as Marlene pulled the door shut.

"Nope. Have you ever contemplated what it might be like to live in San Francisco? Because there's some anemic-looking guy in the outer office who claims you're going to be moving there. My guess is he's a Gemini. I wouldn't trust him any farther than I could spit."

"What?" Alaina crossed the office to peek out the door. Skip Whittaker stood in the center of the reception area, looking around as if he smelled something nasty but was afraid to go looking for the source. She shut the door and stared hard at Marlene. "What did he tell you?"

"He says you're going to blow this podunk town and go back to practicing *real* law. He says you're way too hungry to settle for crumbs when you could be getting a big slice of the financial pie."

Alaina arched a brow. Her voice was cold enough to inflict frostbite. "Oh, really?"

"Yeah. And he doesn't like the wallpaper in the foyer either."

Anger sizzled through Alaina. Real law. As if taking care of the legal needs of the people of Anastasia wasn't worth opening her Louis Vuitton briefcase for. As if the only kind of law that mattered was going for the jugular in a case that meant megabucks and newspaper headlines. Well, that kind of law might have been fine for Horton "Skip" Whittaker III, but she'd had her fill of it.

Marlene chuckled at the arctic-ice gleam in her boss's eyes. "I knew it. The guy's got the aura of a clam."

A malicious smile curved up the corner of Alaina's mouth at the thought of Skip's having Marlene read his aura. His skin was probably still crawling. "Give me a minute, then show Mr. Whittaker in, would you, Marlene?"

"Do I get to watch you shred him to a bloody pulp with your rapier tongue?"

Alaina gave her a look.

Marlene shrugged. "Never hurts to ask."

When Skip sauntered in a moment later, Alaina was cool and composed. Her hair was combed neatly into its fifty-dollar style. Her black-rimmed glasses were perched on her nose. The padded shoulders of her tan Nicole Farhi suit jacket were squared back against her executive chair. She wore a cold smile and an extra spritz of killer French perfume. Adrenaline surged through her at the sight of her old schoolmate. A confrontation like this was precisely what she needed to snap out of her ennui, she decided.

Marlene tucked a smug grin into one corner of her fleshy face. "Buzz me when the dust settles, boss."

Skip frowned and sidled away, his hands toying nervously with the sweater sleeves tied around his neck. Alaina decided he looked like something out of a prep school fashion manual—properly pressed khaki slacks, a white polo shirt with the appropriate reptile embroidered on it, and a bilious-green cable-knit sweater draped over his shoulders. She instantly decided she preferred a man in rumpled chinos and a Bar and Bait Shop T-shirt, but that was beside the point.

"Really, Alaina," Skip drawled, his lip curling in affront. "That secretary of yours is some kind of lunatic. She tried to put her hands on my person! And there are people living in bus depots who dress better. Why do you put up with her?"

"She's my aunt," Alaina said without hesitation, her malicious grin growing as a blush seeped into Skip's pale cheeks. She lit a cigarette and watched him squirm while she stared at him and exhaled smoke. "Let's cut to the chase, Skippy. What brings you to my podunk little town?"

"See, Cleve, I told you that toy company would be a good investment." Dylan tapped a forefinger to the figures glowing on his computer screen. "Their new line of computer games is going to be the hit of the Christmas season."

The big fisherman scratched at his whiskers as he leaned over the polished surface of the bar. "By golly, Dylan, you were right. I owe you. Let me buy you a Kool-Aid."

"Deal."

Stretching cramped shoulder muscles, Dylan pushed away from the terminal and stood up. He pulled off his reading glasses and set them aside as he poured himself a glass of the cherry-red drink he kept on hand for when the kids dropped in to visit him at work.

It was a typical fall afternoon at the bar. A steady stream of locals and tourists kept the waitresses pleasantly busy. The door to the bait shop was opening and closing with profitable regularity as well. All was right with the world.

Then why did he feel so lousy?

A pair of exotic, arctic-blue eyes came immediately to mind. Alaina. Nothing had been the same between them since the trip to San Francisco. She was going to call it quits. He could feel it in his bones. One more item on the agenda of their contract, and he would have no more claim on her time—except for the fact that he was in love with her. All the scowling and snarling he'd done about that in the past few days hadn't changed the fact of the matter. Like it or not, he was in love with Alaina Montgomery, consummate yuppie, and he was damned sick of mooning around about it, longing for the best and fearing the worst.

He wanted more from her. The word *marriage* made him queasy, but that was the direction his heart was headed. He knew the rest of him and all of Alaina had a ways to go before they could broach the subject, but they had to start somewhere. Not breaking up seemed like a logical jumping-off point. The trouble was they had been skidding downhill ever since his foot-in-the-mouth performance at the dinner dance. He'd had no success in trying to show Alaina the error of her yuppie ways. In fact, she'd dug her Gucci pumps in even harder. According to Marlene, she was contemplating trading her Beemer in on a Mercedes, and she was going to have the office redone in a Southwestern motif.

He was going to lose her completely if he didn't do something soon.

Dylan heaved a sigh and turned toward the big fisherman who leaned against the bar, nursing his beer. "Cleve? How do you handle women?"

Cleve stole a glance at his waitress wife to make sure she was out of earshot, then pounded a huge fist on the bar. "You lay down the law. Then you duck, 'cause she's sure to throw something at your head."

"Lay down the law," Dylan mused. It sounded

practical. He and Alaina had certainly done enough pussyfooting around, sniping at each other and pushing each other away when they should have been building on the fire that glowed between them in bed and the friendship they had kindled in saner moments. Lay down the law. Who better to understand the law than a lawyer?

He would tell Alaina exactly how he felt, he thought, his palms breaking out in a cold sweat. And after she finished throwing things at him, they could discuss the possibility of extending their deal. Maybe she wasn't ready for permanence and instant parenthood, but they could take their time moving toward that end. Maybe she'd tell him to take a flying leap, but at least all the cards would be on the table. The idea scared the hell out of him, but Cleve was right. It was time to fish or cut bait. If Alaina didn't want him for something more serious than keeping company, then now was the time to find out, before Cori and Sam got too involved. His own heart was already lost. He was hoping Alaina's was too.

Neither of them had said a word about love. Love hadn't been part of their deal. Love was something both of them had shied away from because of past hurts, but love was what was trying to take root in both their wary hearts. Dylan only hoped he could make Alaina see that. She was a cynic who'd seen nothing but the worst side of relationships. She had turned her nose up at the mention of marriage. But she was also the woman whose eyes were haunted with loneliness and longing, tenderness and vulnerability. Maybe if he had the courage to reach out to her, she would have faith enough to take his hand.

He drank down his Kool-Aid in three big gulps, wiped his mouth with his sleeve, and slammed the glass down on the bar. "Rita, cover for me!" he called.

"Where are you going?" the waitress called back.

"To lay down the law."

A plastic ashtray sailed across the room and bounced off Cleve's head.

Dylan headed up the street from the waterfront, his stride long and purposeful as he passed the picturesque shop fronts of Anastasia. The sun warmed his back through his faded chambray shirt and teased the red and gold lights out in his hair. His battered sneakers ate up the distance between himself and Alaina Montgomery.

When he turned the corner off Main Street and started for the professional building where her office was located, a shiny yellow Mercedes caught his eye and some of the nerve he'd drummed up coagulated in his stomach. His step faltered, but he ignored the omen and flung open the door to the building.

Marlene was leaning down close to her desktop listening intently to her intercom speaker. Her eyes rounded like quarters at the sight of Dylan.

"Can I see Alaina?" he asked.

"Hmmm..." Marlene gave him a shrewd look. "Unless she moves to San Francisco."

Dylan's heart stopped. "Unless what?"

"She's just been offered a position at Victor-Ruthton, the Jaws of California corporate law sharks."

Everything inside him felt as if it had just been freeze-dried. One touch and he would shatter into a zillion shards. Alaina was being offered a position with a prestigious law firm in the city. Alaina, who prized her career and all the perks that accompanied it. Alaina, who valued social status and professional prominence. Alaina, who had stolen his heart despite the fact that she bore no resemblance to Donna Reed.

Pain swirled through him like a hurricane—old pain and new pain, until one was indistinguishable from the other. All the old insecurities Veronica had left him with shot to the surface like heat-seeking missiles. Career women. They were the scourge of the Earth. Didn't love mean anything to them? Was money really more attractive to them than motherhood? Did he have the word *doormat* stenciled across his forehead? He'd come here to throw his heart at Alaina's feet. Now Marlene was telling him he could just as well have left it in San Francisco, because that was where Alaina was headed! When it came down to a choice between fame and fortune and Dylan Harrison, a career woman took the money and ran every time.

Well, he wasn't going to just stand back and wait for her to dump him on her way out of town. Not this time. This time he was going to get his licks in first. This time he was going to be the dumper, not the dumpee.

Without a word to the secretary, he stormed the door to Alaina's office, barging in with a frighteningly false smile on his face. "Skippy!" he crowed, slapping Whittaker on the back hard enough to knock a cough out of him. "Great to see you, Skipster, old pal."

"Dylan!" Alaina gaped at him. Emotions bombarded her like B-52s. There was a thrill at seeing him, a nervousness at the coldness of his brown eyes, and a sliver of anger at having been interrupted in the middle of telling Skip Whittaker to take a long walk off a short pier. "What are you doing here?"

He gave an elaborate shrug. "I just came to tell you your services won't be necessary this Sunday. I can handle the Harrison crowd myself."

Alaina's jaw dropped. He was kissing her off, calling it quits on their deal. Just like that. She sank back in her chair, setting her jaw at an angle maintained by pride alone. "I see," she said softly.

It's really not your kind of scene, anyway," Dylan said, a razor-edge cutting each of his words.

"A Bill Blass gown would be wasted on the Moose Hollow Harrisons."

She flinched a bit at the gibe, but somehow managed to find her voice through the haze of her pain. "So, the deal's off, I take it?"

"Yep. You're free to pack and follow the rainbow to that cushy condo in Marin County, Princess." He leaned across the desk, ruthlessly ignoring the soft allure of her perfume, and tapped a finger to the Crystal pin she wore on the lapel of her jacket. "Give me a call when you decide to part with this. I'd love to have it in my collection."

He turned and started for the door, pausing to flip the ends of Skip's sweater sleeves. "Can't find the neck of your sweater, eh, Skippy? Don't worry. Sweater dyslexia is a temporary learning disability. You'll snap out of it if your gross income dips below fifty grand."

Her breath frozen in her lungs, Alaina watched him walk out. She was stunned. Yes, she'd seen the end coming, but she hadn't expected it to drop out of the sky and land on her like an anvil. Of all the low-down, sneaky strategies! The man was a rat! A brilliant, naturally devious rat! How dare he make her fall in love with him, and then dump her like so much flotsam or jetsam or whatever the hell it was people threw out of boats—ships—

"Hold it right there, buster!" she demanded from the doorway of her office. Dylan turned and stared at her, his dark eyes hard, his jaw set. They faced each other like a pair of gunslingers. Halfway between them, Marlene sat behind her desk, as pale as a corpse. "You can't just say so long and walk out on me."

"Why not?" Dylan questioned, his heart slamming against his chest like a handball. *Because you love me? Because you want me in your life? Because you'd rather have important things than expensive things?*

Alaina stared at him, her heart in her throat. *Because I love you. Because I want you to love me. Because you're the rainbow I've been chasing without even realizing it.* "Because..."

He looked so far away—not just the width of the room away. His heart had left her already. The Dylan who had teased her and tempted her and given her a glimpse of heaven had already gone.

The man facing her was a stranger. The man facing her had hurt her.

She said the first thing that came into her head. "Because you owe me money."

Dylan flinched as though he'd taken a bullet.

"Your tab, you welsher," Alaina said, willing her temper to take over again. "You owe me six hundred seventeen dollars and fifty cents. Plus punitive damages. Plus the twenty-dollar fine I had to pay for creating a public nuisance."

"No way am I paying for that fine!" Dylan bellowed, taking two steps toward her. "You were the one dressed like a hooker!"

Alaina advanced agressively. "You were the one who got us arrested!"

Dylan took the last step so they were nearly nose to nose, temper to temper, hurt to hurt. "You were the one who insulted the deputy!"

From the doorway of Alaina's office, Skip Whittaker called out, "Shall I call security?"

Alaina and Dylan turned on him and shouted in unison, "Butt out, Skippy!"

They faced each other once again, both of them in pain, but neither willing to back down.

"Okay, Counselor," Dylan murmured, his eyes locked on hers. "A deal's a deal. Send me the bill. I'll send you a check. Take it to bed with you at night and see if it keeps you warm."

It was Alaina's turn to wince. Was that really what he thought of her? That she valued nothing so much as a dollar? He of the thirty-foot fishing boat and the one-of-a-kind collection and the state-of-the-art telescope. "You smug, self-righteous, hypocritical bastard. Keep your damn money. Frame it and hang it on the wall. Send it to the starving people in Ethiopia. Stick it where the sun don't shine. I don't want anything from you."

"Yeah. You've made that plain enough. Have a nice life at the top of the corporate ladder, Princess." He raised his arm in a proper Zanatarian salute and backed toward the door. "It's been real."

The instant he was gone, Alaina felt all the strength rush out of her like bathwater down a drain. She sagged back against Marlene's desk, unable to believe what had just happened. She'd just verbally duked it out with Dylan. He'd thrown her out of his life, and she'd thrown him out of her office. She felt disoriented, as if she'd just been thrust into a bizarre nightmare. This was even weirder than Dylan's entrance into her life had been.

From the doorway Whittaker gave an indignant snort. "You're well rid of him, Alaina. The man is obviously unstable."

She narrowed her eyes and glared at him. "Put a cork in it, Skippy."

Chapter 11

"Have you been reading a lot of Stephen King novels recently?"

Alaina paused with her brush poised above the canvas. She shot Faith Kincaid a suspicious look. "No. Why?"

Faith leaned back on the porch swing, her arms wrapped around her drawn-up knees. A pained smile tilted the corners of her small mouth. The huge brown eyes that dominated her heart-shaped face were full of concern. "No reason. Your painting just seems a little ... grimmer than usual."

Turning a critical eye toward the canvas that

was propped on the easel, Jayne nibbled on a croissant and made a face. She tucked a wild strand of auburn hair behind her ear. " 'Grim' is a good word."

"Everybody's a critic," Alaina grumbled, slapping another glob of black onto the mess she'd created. Splashes of dark red and black warred for space on the canvas. Originally, she had intended to attempt painting another horse—one that didn't look like a deformed dog. But the emotions she had been trying to lock inside for the past three days had conducted themselves down her arm and out the end of her paintbrush. Privately she called the result *The Futility of Love*. All things considered, it seemed an accurate portrayal of her feelings.

"What do you call it?" Jayne asked.

"Men Are Pond Scum." She took a long, last drag on her eighth cigarette of the morning, stubbed it out on the Limoges saucer that sat on the small wicker table, and promptly lit another.

Jayne and Faith exchanged worried glances.

"How was Maine?" Alaina asked, uncomfortable with the feel of eyes boring into her back.

"Fine. Shane's family was very nice. They're all going to make it out for the wedding," Faith said. She declined the chocolate doughnut Jayne offered her, paling delicately.

Wedding. Alaina grimaced. Lord, how was she going to endure a wedding? All those people gushing over the power of love and the glow of the happy couple. But get through it she would. She loved Faith like a sister, and she certainly didn't begrudge her friend this ultimate happiness. After what she'd had to endure with her first husband, Faith deserved the kind of love she had with Shane Callan.

It was just that...

"Since when do you turn down chocolate doughnuts?" Jayne asked, licking the last of the frosting from her fingertips.

Faith's cheeks turned a lovely shade of pink. Her lashes fluttered down shyly. "Since morning sickness."

Lovely. Just lovely, Alaina thought as a lump the size of a softball ballooned to life in her throat. She muttered curses at the hot moisture that burned the backs of her eyeballs. Dammit, she would not cry because Faith was pregnant. She would not cry because Faith was finding the end of a rainbow while she was getting drenched in yet another downpour of romantic disappointment.

Who needed pregnancy anyway? Nausea and swelling body parts she could get from one good helping of lobster Newburg.

Lindy Kincaid crawled out from under the porch with dirt on her pink overalls and leaves clinging to her rusty-gold curls. The four-year-old scrambled up the porch steps, her dark eyes shining and a delighted smile on her pixie face. Alaina had to quell the urge to scoop the child up and run off with her.

"Mama!" Lindy called excitedly. "There's kitties under here! Come see!"

I'm doomed, Alaina thought morosely as she fell in line behind her friends. Lindy led the way down the steps, then crouched down in the impossible way of children and pointed under the porch. Sure enough, there lay Julia looking smug and superior as three parti-colored kittens nursed at her side.

"That does it," Alaina mumbled fatalistically.

She sat down on the porch steps with a *thump*, bracing her elbows on her knees and plunking her head in her hands.

Since Dylan's departure from her life—no, since before Dylan's departure; hell, all her life—she'd been telling herself she didn't need a family, that she didn't want a man in her life, that she could rely on no one but herself. And all the while on a deeper level, a level where a lonely little girl had grown into a lonely woman, she had always longed for just those things. Now they had been within her grasp and had slipped away. Or had they been snatched away? Or had she pushed them away?

What did it matter? The dream had eluded her and life was taunting her with her failure. Faith was getting married. Faith had a beautiful daughter and a baby on the way. Even the damn cat had a family!

The telephone rang, and Alaina hauled herself onto the porch and snatched up the cordless receiver from the wicker table. She yanked out the phone's antenna and growled into the mouthpiece, "Speak now or forever hold your peace."

The polished voice that sailed over the lines set her teeth on edge. "Alaina, darling, it's Helene. Your mother. Wonderful news, dear. I'm getting married again!"

Without a word, Alaina took the phone from her ear and dropped it into the pitcher of orange juice sitting on the breakfast tray. Faith and Jayne stared at her, biting their lips.

"I'm going for a walk," she announced, descending the steps like a queen. "If I never come back, you may divide my possessions equally among yourselves and run over Dylan Harrison with my car."

"Marlene mentioned the two of you had a little tiff," Jayne said. She nibbled nervously on a purple-polished fingernail. "You're really mad at him, huh?"

"Mad?" she questioned softly. "He roped me into an alleged no-strings relationship, made me fall in love with him, then decided I was just too ambitious and materialistic for his pious, reformed tastes."

Jayne winced.

Alaina pressed on, lifting a slender finger to

emphasize her point. "You know, if there's one thing I hate even more than a reformed smoker, it's a reformed yuppie. Dylan Harrison is a pompous, self-righteous hypocrite. He's a conniving con man and a welsher. I hope all his hair falls out. I hope his teeth turn black, and his neighbors raze their house, pour asphalt on the lawn, and open a Kmart. Does that answer your question?"

"In spades."

Alaina crossed her arms in front of her defensively. "Well? Aren't you going to say it? Aren't you going to say I told you so?" Lord knew she'd been waiting to hear it. She'd thought she was so darn smart cooking up this scheme with Dylan to get out of all those wretched blind dates Jayne and Marlene had pushed her into. They'd crowed all along about incompatibility. So why weren't they crowing now? "Well?"

Jayne looked distinctly uneasy. In fact, she looked downright guilty. "Umm . . . can I plead the Fifth Amendment?"

"Jayne." Faith planted her hands on her hips and gave their flaky friend her sternest mother look. "What have you done?"

"I just thought you two were so right for each other!" Jayne wailed, turning beseeching eyes on Alaina.

Alaina's jaw dropped so that she nearly impaled it on the point of the Crystal pin she was wearing at the throat of her burgundy blouse. "You what?! No, don't tell me," she demanded, holding up a hand to ward off Jayne's explanation. "You were matchmaking. You made me go out with all those dorks just so I'd think Dylan was a prize. You're Marlene's apprentice wizard or something."

"I just wanted you and Dylan to be happy. I've never known two people more alike. Oh, I know y'all have different taste in clothes and things, but deep down you're both stubborn and opinionated and smart and dedicated"—Jayne's night-dark eyes filled with tears—"and lonely."

Alaina stepped back as if she'd been slapped. Her face paled to the color of parchment. Jayne had set her up because she thought she was lonely. Lord, had she really sunk to this? Pity from one of her dearest friends.

"I think I'll take that walk now," she whispered, and turned away.

Jayne bit her lip and sniffled as she watched Alaina pause halfway down the sidewalk to collect her mail from the mailman. "You don't think she'll do anything crazy, do you?"

Faith stared after their friend as well, her expression sad and sympathetic. "No. Alaina's tough. Besides, she'd never do anything to ruin her outfit—it's Ralph Lauren."

She sat on the beach, just out of reach of the waves. Gulls swooped and called overhead. Farther up the sand, people gathered in knots of two or three, enjoying the last of the warm weather, laughing and talking and soaking up the Saturday-morning sun. But Alaina sat alone, apart, as she had always been. The shield of separateness she'd developed so long ago still surrounded her, keeping people out, keeping her safe.

No. That was a lie. It hadn't kept her safe from Dylan. He'd barged into her life like a whirlwind. He'd touched her and he'd hurt her and damned

309

if she didn't still love him. Brother, that ticked her off. She'd been ready to give her heart to him on a platter. She'd been ready to sign up for cooking lessons. And what had he done? Jumped to the conclusion that she would take a partnership at Victor-Ruthton over a partnership with him.

Maybe his first wife would have made that choice, maybe it was his first wife's love for things that had frightened him into dumping her. But she wasn't Veronica Howard. She was Alaina Montgomery, and she loved *him,* the boneheaded man. She liked her career and her clothes and her BMW, but she *loved* Dylan Harrison. She'd never gotten the chance to tell him. She'd never taken a chance and told him.

Why quibble over wording now? It was too late. She was too hurt and too proud to go crawling back to him, and he was too stubborn and too pigheaded to come crawling back to her. She had lost him. Lord, how she hated losing!

To distract herself, she picked up her mail and shuffled through it. There was the usual assortment of bills and charity requests. At the bottom of the pile was a packet postmarked Scotland.

Knowing it would be from Bryan Hennessy, she tore the envelope open and extracted a paperback book that had seen better days. *Tales of the Kalamari* by Frank D. Richard. On the cover was an artist's rendering of the Crystal pin she wore, bursting with color. Beneath it was an excerpt: "If your heart is pure and your desire strong, the Crystal can make your dreams come true. Believe."

Inside the cover Bryan had jotted a message in pencil: *Somewhere out there is a rainbow with your name on it. Believe. Love, Bryan.*

"I don't think so, friend," Alaina whispered as she stood up and unpinned the Crystal from her blouse.

She was all through with rainbows. Chasing them left her nothing but exhausted, disillusioned, and soul-weary. She stared down at the prism of glass in her hand for one long last moment, then threw it into the sea.

The surf promptly washed it up at her feet.

Alaina scowled at the pin and picked it up. "Look, you cheap piece of glass, I've had it with you and your phony promises. Maybe my heart isn't entirely pure, but I sure as hell desired Dylan Harrison, and you didn't deliver. I ought to sue for breach of contract. I ought to—"

She cut herself off abruptly as wheels started turning in her head. "That's it," she whispered, her heart suddenly pounding. "That's it!"

The Harrison family reunion was an annual affair that moved up and down the Pacific coast from Seattle to San Francisco, depending upon whose turn it was to host the event. Every year Harrisons came from Washington, Oregon, and California, gathering together to eat and talk sports and reminisce and try to marry off the single members of the family.

It was Dylan's year to host, and it was his year to be singled out as the prime male ripe for matrimony. By noon he'd lost track of the female friends of cousins who had been paraded before him. Once he'd sought refuge in a game of touch football with his brothers, only to be tackled by a gang of eligible ladies. It was embarrassing. It was depressing.

Alaina was the woman he wanted. She was the one he had intended to introduce to all his matchmaking aunts. He missed her. He was downright miserable not having her around to spar with and tease. He hadn't had a wink of sleep since their fight because he'd been lying awake all night, aching to hold her. She was the last woman he should have wanted. She was the only woman his heart desired. And it was over between them. He'd seen to that. In the face of a challenge where she might have chosen him over her career, he'd jumped right in there and given her a great big shove out of his life.

He sat on a little sand dune a few feet away from the main crowd, having successfully snuck away for a moment of peace and self-pity. There were Harrisons all over the beach, all of them having a disgustingly good time. Even Mrs. Pepoon looked animated as she explained to his Aunt Ruth how to use common household spray starch to style hair into a proper beehive.

Cori wandered up the sand dune and plopped down on his lap, looking up at him with big, somber brown eyes. "I'm sad."

Dylan brushed her bangs back with a gentle hand. "What are you sad about?"

"I'm sad 'cause you're sad."

He wrapped his arms around his little girl and hugged her, thankful to have such wonderful children and the time to love them.

Sam jogged up and stopped in front of them, his expression even more serious than usual. Two of his young cousins lingered a few feet behind him, wide-eyed as they stared at Dylan.

"Dad, will Cori and I be able to visit you during your unfortunate incarceration in the penitentiary?"

"They call it the slammer," cousin Mickey whispered to cousin Greg.

Greg looked sideways at Dylan. "What did he do, off somebody? Maybe he's going undercover. I saw that on *Wiseguy*. Think they'll put him in solitary confinement?"

"The box," Mickey murmured, moon-eyed.

"Prison?" Dylan's brows drew together as he stared at the boys. "I'm not going to prison."

"We'll just see about that, bub." Deputy Skreawupp hooked his thumbs behind his belt buckle and glared down at Dylan, his eyes narrowed to beady little slits in his fleshy face. "You're in big trouble, and if you try anything, I'll tear you up like a wet newspaper."

Dylan set Cori down and pushed himself to his feet, brushing sand from the seat of his jeans. "What's this all about?"

"Breach of contract," Alaina announced, stepping around the deputy. She wore her glasses and a stylish gray suit and carried a sheaf of papers in one hand and her Gucci pumps in the other. She'd pulled her hair back and secured it at the nape of her neck, but the sea breeze had already pulled tendrils loose and brushed them around her face.

Dylan stared at her, torn between joy and fury. What was she up to? Was she so steamed at him she'd really sic the law on him for that lousy twenty-dollar fine? Or was this about something else altogether?

Alaina swallowed back a major lump of nerves as she looked up at Dylan. What if she was way off base, and he just plain didn't want her hanging around? What if she was right, and he was as in love with her as she was with him? It seemed well worth risking humiliation in front of a hundred and fifty Harrisons to find out. The entire clan had gathered around to witness the confrontation. She'd never dreamed there'd be so many of them.

"Breach of contract," she repeated, dropping her shoes to page through the document she'd brought with her. Scottie the dog dodged through the sea of legs to snatch one suede pump between his teeth. Alaina watched him run off, but made no comment. Turning back to her document, she took a deep breath and plunged in. "This is a written copy of the verbal agreement struck between the accused, Dylan Henry Harrison, and the plaintiff, Alaina N. Montgomery. It clearly states that Mr. Harrison agreed to—indeed instigated— a relationship and has since reneged on that agreement, causing the plaintiff to suffer emotional distress, i.e."—she cleared her throat and went for broke—"a broken heart."

Warmth flooded through Dylan like the rays of the sun breaking over the horizon after a long dark night. He'd broken her heart. That had to mean she had committed her heart, that keeping company had meant more to her than an easy date.

Alaina stole a glance up at him and took hope at the soft shine in his dark eyes. She gulped a breath of air and went on. "Additional charges are: reckless endangerment of the emotions, being a jerk, bombastic pomposity, and jumping to erroneous conclusions."

Dylan squeezed his eyes shut and cursed himself for being an impulsive reactionary imbecile even though Alaina hadn't put that on the list. "You weren't going to take that job at Vicious-Ruthless?"

Pulling her glasses off, she looked up at him with her heart in her eyes. Her low voice was as soft as the sea breeze that carried it to him. "Why would I when everything I ever wanted is right here waiting for me?"

Dylan didn't see the throng of relatives gathered around them, gawking. He saw only Alaina. Alaina with no shield of sardonic wit, no barrier of cool self-possession. He saw her as he had dreamed of seeing her—with her blue eyes full of love and hope. He took a step closer and reached out to run his fingertips over her cheek.

"I enjoy my career, Dylan, but it's not my whole life," she said. "Maybe it was once, but I left that attitude when I left Chicago. I want other things besides professional success. I want a husband and a family. I want it all." Her lush lower lip pouted out just a tad as she frowned prettily. "Maybe that's being greedy, but there it is. What do you expect? I am from the me generation. And so are you, Captain Consumer, with your fishing boat and your closet investment counseling."

"I'm a jerk," Dylan murmured in the low, resonant voice that brushed against Alaina's nerve endings like velvet. "I'm a grade-A jerk."

"Didn't I mention that?"

"So you did, Counselor," he said with a soft smile. "The question is, what are you going to do about it? Beat me with your Gucci handbag? Stick slivers of gold charge cards under my fingernails?"

"Actually, I thought about having a truckload of fertilizer dumped in your living room, and I thought about sneaking into your bedroom and shaving all your body hair off as you slept. I contemplated turning live pigs loose on your ship, and I briefly considered sending your address to the mailing list of a male escort service."

Dylan winced even as he stepped closer and slid his arms around her. The lady had a creatively vindictive mind. He would have to remember to stay on her good side from now on. "Couldn't we work something out contractually? I'd be more than willing to meet your terms."

"You don't know what my terms are."

"Name them."

She looked at him for a long moment, clutching her legal briefs to her chest. Her heart was going a hundred miles an hour. She wondered briefly if Deputy Screwup knew CPR. Oh, what the hell, she thought, go for broke. No guts, no glory.

"Love me," she whispered, her gaze locked on Dylan's as if she could will him to feel that emotion that had taken her over. "I love you. I want you to love me back."

"I love you already," he admitted with a gentle smile. "Couldn't you tell?"

"You have a funny way of showing it. You told me to move to San Francisco."

His broad shoulders lifted and fell in resignation. "So I'm a lunatic."

Alaina rolled her eyes. "I've known that from the beginning. I probably should have maced you when I had the chance."

"Probably," he agreed with a grin, "but you're stuck with me now. It's a deal—on one condition."

Alaina eyed him warily. He suddenly looked very grave.

"You have to tell me what the *N* stands for."

A gasp accompanied her horrified grimace. "Brother, you play hardball."

He nodded, looking very much like a pirate with his gold earring and wolfish grin and the wind riffling his unruly dark hair. All he needed was an eye patch and a parrot. "Come on, Princess. A deal's a deal. Spill it."

Alaina made a face that looked as if she'd just been forced to swallow something vile, then she heaved a sigh and stood up on her tiptoes to whisper in his ear. "Nanette. And if you *ever* utter that in public, I'll pull all your toenails out with pliers."

Dylan laughed and hugged her. "Don't worry. I plan to use it only in an intimate setting. I won't hold it against you. I'd rather hold me against you."

She slanted him a look. "You're completely irreverent."

"But is he under arrest?" Deputy Skreawupp demanded to know.

A wry smile slanted Alaina's lush mouth as she looked up at the culprit who'd stolen her heart. "Not this time, Deputy. I'm dropping the charges."

Disgruntled over losing the bust, Deputy Skreawupp assumed the job of crowd control, herding the curious Harrisons away. "Break it up, folks. The show's over. Go back to your activities. Don't give me any guff, or I'll snap you like dry twigs."

"You could put me under house arrest," Dylan murmured, nuzzling his lips against the satin softness of Alaina's.

"Now there's an idea," she whispered, dropping her documents to the sand so she could get closer to Dylan. He was warm and solid and curved in all the right places.

"Confine me to quarters," he said dramatically. "Chain me to my bed. I can handle it." His eyes took on a dangerous gleam, and he leered at her. "Better yet, you can handle it for me."

Alaina swatted his arm. "Will you get serious?"

Dylan sobered in an instant as he lifted a big hand to brush her hair back from her face. She was so lovely, and he loved her so much. "I am serious—about you. I love you. That scares me, which is why I made such a mess of things. I know we have a way to go, Princess, but I'd really like to make this deal a permanent one. What do you say? Think you could get into domestic bliss?"

She looked down at the Crystal pinned to the lapel of her jacket and smiled softly at the colors that glowed inside it. "I'd say maybe this silly thing works after all."

She turned her smile to Dylan, and he answered it with one of his own. And in the absence of a notary, they sealed the deal with a kiss.